ALSO BY Donna Schwartze

The Only Reason (The Trident Trilogy: Book Two)
Wild Card (The Trident Trilogy: Book Three)

Eight Years is the first book of The Trident Trilogy.

Buy the other two books, *The Only Reason* and *Wild Card*, on Amazon.

EIGHT YEARS
(THE TRIDENT TRILOGY: BOOK ONE)

DONNA SCHWARTZE

ISBN: 9798655419322

Published by Donna Schwartze, 2020

donnaschwartzeauthor@gmail.com

❀ Created with Vellum

EIGHT YEARS

(The Trident Trilogy: Book One)

DONNA SCHWARTZE

For my dad, whose gentle spirit has guided me through this life.

"Failing to fetch me at first keep encouraged, Missing me one place search another, I stop somewhere waiting for you."

— *Walt Whitman, "Song of Myself"*

Prologue

SARAJEVO, BOSNIA, 1995

The baby was howling when he approached the door. He quickly picked the lock and found her lying on a blanket in the middle of the dark one-room apartment. Putting his gun back in his waistband, he picked her up and walked out the door. He passed three people on the way out of the building. No one challenged him.

When the flight attendant leaned down to talk to him before takeoff, he thought he had been caught.

"She looks just like you, especially with that pretty red hair," she said.

He took a deep breath and let himself smile for the first time in a month.

Chapter One

Camille gasped when she opened the door and saw her son standing there. She hadn't seen or talked to him since he left for the navy five years ago. She barely recognized him. When he left at eighteen, he had been a skinny, gawkish boy. The man who stood before her now bore no resemblance to that boy except for his deep auburn hair that had unfortunately become a constant reminder of his absent father.

Mack had added at least fifty pounds of muscle to his six-foot frame. His once neatly clipped hair was now wildly over-grown. He had an unhealed gash that started at his left eye and zigzagged down his face until it disappeared into his scraggly, unkept beard. Tattoos now sprouted out of every opening of his T-shirt.

"Camille," Mack said calmly as he walked past her into the house, leaving her standing on the porch, her mouth and eyes gaping.

Camille watched him from the safety of the porch as he unapologetically sat down on her immaculate couch in his filthy clothes. When he was growing up, Camille would have put him over her knee for breaking one of her cardinal rules. That wasn't going to be possible anymore.

"Are you coming in?" Mack said, his voice an unusual combination of impatience and amusement.

Camille tentatively followed him into the room, making sure to leave the front door open.

"What are you doing here, Mack?" Camille said, trying to keep her voice calm to gain back some control over the situation.

"I'm here to introduce you to your granddaughter." Mack stood up and walked toward her, slightly unzipping a backpack that was strapped to his chest to reveal an infant's head.

Camille took a step away from him, holding her hands up to try to shield herself from the fact that she was now a grandmother. Mack smiled and shook his head. It was about the response he expected from her. She had never been a big fan of children, especially her own.

Camille had gotten pregnant at sixteen from a one-night stand with a boy who had been vacationing in the Outer Banks with his family. By the time she found out she was pregnant, he was long gone, leaving behind only a fake name and phone number. She blamed Mack for that his entire life.

Camille walked quickly past Mack into the kitchen, ignoring the news that she was a grandmother. "You look horrible, Mack. Does the navy not make you groom? Or did you get kicked out?"

"I'm still in the navy, Camille."

"And, the navy allows you to run around looking like that," she said, waving her hands at him.

"I'm in the special forces. We can look however we want."

"Dr. Tripp told me you had made it into some special outfit. He wouldn't quit talking about it, like it was something out of the ordinary."

Mack didn't say anything. He'd never had his mother's approval, and he'd stopped seeking it a long time ago. He knew that even becoming a SEAL would not impress her.

Holding the baby, Mack walked over to stand next to Camille. "Camille, this is Millie. Her mother died in child-birth, and I'm the only thing she has left. I can't keep her because I'm on active duty. I need you to help me out. I need you to keep her."

Camille looked like someone had just thrown a pot of boiling water in her face. There was no way she wanted to raise another baby. She hadn't even wanted to raise Mack.

"Absolutely not," she said, picking up a knife to start cutting up the watermelon she had picked from her garden that morning.

"Camille, I've never asked anything of you in my entire life. I need you to do this for me."

"Well, she's at least three months old," Camille said, walking away from the baby's outstretched arms. "If her momma died in childbirth, someone has been watching her since then."

"I already told you she doesn't have anyone left on that side of the family. She was in foster care when I found out about her." Camille had never been able to tell when Mack was lying, and he had only gotten better at it since he left home.

"Well, maybe she should just stay in foster care. It might be the best thing for her."

"Camille, she's your granddaughter." Mack almost laughed as he said it. He knew that was the weakest argument he could make.

"Are you sure? Do you even know for sure she's your daughter?"

"She's my daughter, Camille." Mack tried to keep his tone civil, but he was due back at the base tomorrow. He was desperate.

"Well, then maybe you should take care of her. I haven't seen you in five years, and now you show up here, expecting me to take care of your baby."

"Camille, I can't just quit the navy. I've already been away from my team for two weeks. I have to go back. I'll come to see Millie every chance I get. It's less than two years until my enlistment is up."

In reality, Mack couldn't imagine leaving his team. It had been his entire life until he found out about the baby. But his training had taught him to deal with one problem at a time. He'd worry about the rest in two years. Right now, he just needed a place to hide Millie.

He breathed deeply, and finally played his last card. "If you take her in, I'll start sending you half of my paycheck every month."

Mack knew Camille needed the money. Her parents— whom he had never met—had been sending her a monthly stipend since Mack was born. He liked to think it was out of the goodness of their hearts, but he later found out it was hush money. They had been paying her to hide Mack in the Outer Banks—far from the prying eyes and ears of their hometown in Raleigh. He heard from Camille's friend, Beatrice, that they had stopped paying when Mack turned eighteen.

Millie started to stir. Her curly red hair was damp from being zipped up in the baby carrier. She rubbed her head back and forth against Mack's broad chest and then looked up at him—her sparkling green eyes starting to fill with tears. Camille watched as Mack grabbed a bottle out of the backpack and took the cap off with his teeth. He held the bottle to her lips. She shook her head in refusal, and cried harder.

"Oh for God's sake, Mack, heat the bottle up first. Give it to me," Camille said as she grabbed the bottle and stuck it in the microwave. "And, it smells like she needs a change. Do you have any diapers, and do you know how to change one?"

Mack didn't bother telling her that he had flown almost five thousand miles with Millie in the last week. He needed Camille to feel like she was in charge again. Camille took Millie from Mack's arms and put her on the day-bed off the kitchen to change her. Mack brought a diaper and baby wipes in to her just in time to see Millie cooing up at Camille, bubbles coming out of her mouth. Although Camille wasn't smiling, he could tell she had changed her mind. He wanted to think it was because Millie was winning her over, but he knew it was more about the money.

"What's her full name?" Camille said as she picked Millie up and took her back into the kitchen to feed her.

"Her full name is Millicent Mackenzie Marsh." Mack had

gotten her a birth certificate when they got back in the country. He had no idea what her mother had named her, if anything.

"I like the name Millicent better than Millie. It sounds more dignified. That's what I'm going to call her," Camille said. "And, I'll take her for two years until you get out of the navy, and then I'm done."

"I know Millie is not your responsibility, and I really do appreciate you looking after her for me," Mack said.

Camille was happy that the balance of power had shifted back her way. "Your crib is still up in the attic if you want to set it up for her before you leave."

Mack spent the rest of the day setting up his old room for Millie, and stocking the house with baby supplies. He got her to sleep in her new crib, and went downstairs to find Camille cooking dinner. Amazingly, it seemed that she was making enough for two.

"I'm leaving you five hundred dollars to start with. I'll send you more next week." Mack put five crisp one hundred dollar bills on the kitchen table. He saw Camille eyeing them hungrily.

"I'm making dinner if you want some," she offered in a less snarky tone than usual.

"That would be nice. Thank you." For all her faults, Camille was a great cook, and the smell of fried chicken had Mack's stomach doing flip-flops.

Camille placed a large plate of chicken, and a bowl of mashed potatoes right in front of him. "Two years, Mack. And, you need to come down here and give me breaks whenever you can."

He nodded affirmatively, his mouth already full of food. He wasn't at all ready for the responsibility of having a baby, but he knew already that he'd spend every second of his downtime here. He had fallen in love with Millie the minute he had seen her lying in the middle of that tiny apartment.

Chapter Two

Chase is persistent. I'll give him that. In the past eight years, I've changed my address three times and my phone number five times. I've lived in three different cities. He's found me every time. This last time it took him a while though—almost three years. I know what tipped him off. I knew it would when I did it. But, it had to be done.

I'm rereading the yet-unanswered text he sent me last night when I hear, "Millie?" For a split second, I think it's him. But when I look up, I see a guy from my high school smiling so broadly at me that I think his face might break.

"Heeeeeeeeeeey," I say, stretching out the word as far as possible as I try to remember his name.

"Will. Will Peters. I was a year younger than you in high school."

"Of course. I'm sorry, you caught me off guard."

Living in D.C. now, I rarely run into anyone from back home. Even though it's just a four-hour drive down the coast,

D.C. and the Outer Banks might as well be on two different planets.

"So, wow, do you live in D.C. now? I never see you around The OB anymore."

God, I used to hate when people called it that. Apparently, I still do.

"Yeah, I haven't been back in a while."

Unfortunately, Will starts to give me a play-by-play of what's been happening back home since I left. Thankfully, my always punctual boyfriend shows up just in time to save me.

"Hey, babe." Drew kisses me on the cheek before walking right in front of Will to take the seat across the table from me. I'm guessing he thinks Will is the waiter.

"Is this your husband?" Will says, extending his hand to Drew.

"Boyfriend. This is Drew. Drew, Will and I went to high school together," I say, giving Drew a warning look across the table. He knows I hate talking about my childhood.

"Ohhhhh, high school. Millie talks nonstop about those days." Drew's voice is dripping with sarcasm that Will obviously doesn't pick up on.

"Yeah, man, best years of our lives. Right, Mills?"

I kick Drew under the table to try to get him to control the smile that's now about to burst off of his face.

"Yep, those were the days," I say.

Honestly, I did have a great time in high school. Amazing time. But with everything that's happened since then, I've tried—and mainly succeeded—to block that time from my mind. It's the only way I've been able to survive.

"Millie, I never got a chance to tell you how sorry I was

about your grandma and dad dying—especially that close together. That had to be tough," Will says.

Drew stops smiling. That's something else I don't talk to him about. I've been dating him for almost two years, and the amount of information I've been able to keep from him is almost shocking. It helps that he's not a very curious person.

"Thank you, Will," I say with a forced smile. "It's been really nice seeing you again. Take care of yourself."

"Yeah, yeah, you too," Will says, finally taking a few steps away from the table. "You still look amazing, Mills. Just like that beach babe from high school. I guess D.C. hasn't changed you that much."

Thankfully, it's changed me completely. The old Millie couldn't have survived.

As Will walks away, I look back to see Drew's disappointed face. "Really? I have to find out that your dad and your grandma are dead from Bill?"

"Will. His name is Will."

"Millie, do I give a fuck what Mr. High School's name is? Why didn't I know that? We've been dating for two years. You don't talk about yourself enough."

Well, that's just the understatement of the year.

"Hey. How's everybody tonight? A few cocktails before dinner?" The waiter has perfect timing.

Drew gives me the "we're not done with this conversation" look, and grabs the wine list. I know we probably are done though. In addition to not having much curiosity, Drew's also easily distracted.

The waiter walks away to get our Pinot Noir. Before Drew

can start asking any more uncomfortable questions, I say, "So tell me about the Jackson Unlimited case. Any progress?"

Drew's a corporate attorney, and amazingly he can—and does—talk about it for hours. I never talk about my work. I can't. I work for the CIA. Drew thinks I work for the State Department. It's a good cover for why I travel so much. Drew's a good guy, but I know there's no real future with him. It's almost impossible to have a healthy relationship with someone you have to lie to every day. He's a great companion, a great plus-one, but I know when all of this is over, I'm going to end up breaking his heart. I don't feel good about it, but frankly, there's a lot I do in my day that I don't feel very good about. It's all a means to an end. I won't be at peace until I find out the truth. That's my only focus now, and no one—not even Drew—is going to get in the way.

Drew has just ended his lengthy summation about his current case. "So, Bill-Will said you were a beach babe in high school, huh? I don't think I've ever seen you touch a beach."

"Well, considering we live in D.C., unless you think the Potomac is an ocean, you're probably never going to see me on one."

"We should take a vacation. Maybe go back and visit the Outer Banks. I'd like to see where you grew up," he says hopefully.

That's never going to happen. Never. There's more chance of me spilling all my secrets to him.

"Yeah, maybe. You know I travel so much for work, I kind of like to stay around here when I can."

"I know. I know," Drew says, sighing. "When are you out next?"

"In a few days or so. Not sure of the timing exactly."

Actually, I haven't even presented my next proposed target package to my boss. It's a solid one though, and he's never been very good at saying no to me. Getting his permission is really more of a formality at this point.

"Are you going overseas?" Drew asks, knowing to keep his questions vague if he wants them answered at all.

"Yeah, and I'm not sure for how long. It could be a while."

"Your travel schedule is so unpredictable. I don't know how you deal with it."

Drew starts telling me about a new client he just signed today. I smile and nod at the appropriate moments, but my mind is back on the text from Chase. I'm not sure how to answer it or even if I should. He knows where I am now and, more importantly, where I'm headed: back to Virginia Beach, the last place I saw him. I've avoided it successfully for so many years, but I know now that the road to the truth has to go right through there. The thought of going back fills me with a sense of dread that I haven't experienced in a long time. The memories I had almost shut down completely are already starting to resurface, and I know they're going to blow up the minute I cross the city line.

What do they say? Sometimes things have to get worse before they can get better. Well, things are about to get a whole lot worse, and if this all ends like I think it will, things are definitely not going to get better.

Chapter Three

MASON, VIRGINIA BEACH, VIRGINIA, 2019

"Fuck," I say to no one as I look in my empty refrigerator. You'd think after fifteen years of doing this, I'd have at least learned to leave a little bit of beer in there.

My ex always had the fridge completely stocked when I got back from deployment. She'd have dinner waiting for me with an ample supply of beer. It was great until I got done eating, and she wanted to talk. That's the last thing I wanted to do. I just wanted to sit on my couch, drink beer, and watch sports. We were only married two years when she asked me for a divorce. It didn't surprise me. It didn't really even upset me. And believe me, that says way more about me than it does about her.

I'm contemplating how bad three-month-old leftover pizza might taste when I hear someone at my door. With what I do for a living, I never trust a random knock at the door. I look through the peephole and see a woman holding a plate and a six-pack. There are worse things to see, especially right now.

"Hey," she says as I open the door. "It's me. Rebecca. I moved in next door right before you left on deployment. Remember? You helped me carry my TV in."

I kind of remembered. "Oh yeah, right. Hey."

"I saw you in the parking lot earlier. I figured you just got back and could maybe use something to eat—and drink. I made lasagna if you want some." She lifts the plate up closer to my face. It smells so good.

"Oh man, that's really nice," I say as I accept the food and beer while trying to figure out how to politely indicate that's all I want from her.

Before I can, she's taken the plate back from me and deftly moved herself through the small opening between me and the door. "Here, I'll heat it up for you," she says.

I stand at the door for a second, trying to think of a way to get out of this, but I'm tired and hungry. My defenses are down. I head to the couch, popping open one of the beers on the way. She's saying something from the kitchen. I'm not listening. I turn up *SportsCenter* to drown her out.

"I brought you some garlic bread, too," she says as she hands me the plate. "I didn't know if you'd eat salad. Do you eat salad? I mean, you're in great shape, but you look like more of a meat-and-potatoes guy."

I inhale the food, washing it down with my third beer. I'm not saying anything to her, but she's still talking. And she keeps edging closer to me on the couch. Jesus, I know how she wants me to repay her. I mean, she's good-looking and all, but I don't lack for female companionship, even on deployment.

It's crazy to me how women chase us. They hunt us down

like we're exotic animals in a safari. Most of us are just about as exotic as that old penny you pass over in the parking lot. But I guess what we do for a living makes us seem dangerous. If that turns women on, hey, I'm not complaining. It's a great fantasy for one night.

Rebecca rubs my shoulders as I try to keep a razor-sharp focus on the TV.

"Do you want a back rub? I could do your entire back if you want to lay down," she whispers into my ear.

Fuck. Okay, let's get this over with. I turn to kiss her. She responds like an animal that's been caged for months. She jumps on my lap, almost spilling my beer. I manage to set it down on the floor before she starts pulling off my T-shirt. The first thing she sees is—the first thing they all see—the scar on my shoulder where I took my first bullet. I've been hit several times, but that one kept me out of action for almost six months. I don't like talking about it, and they always want to talk about it.

"Oh, what happened here?" she says, running her finger over the scar.

Before she can talk anymore, I flip her onto her back and reach under her skirt to pull off her underwear. She's not wearing any. Well, at least that requires less effort on my part. I don't bother taking off my jeans. This is going to be fast. I unzip, grab a condom off the table, and am inside her in seconds. Yeah, I keep condoms on the table. I don't mean to sound like an asshole, but this happens a lot.

She starts saying something again, so I go back to kissing her until I'm ready to cum. She makes a sound underneath me as I collapse on top of her. I lay there for a second, catching my breath before I pull out. I go to the bathroom to throw away the condom. When I walk back in the room, she's still laying on the couch.

"Hey, I appreciate the lasagna. It was good," I say. "You want me to wash the plate before I return it?"

She's sitting up now, looking at me with the expression they always have. I'm not sure what they expect.

"Um, no, I can just take it," she says slowly.

I hand her the plate and open the door. "Thanks again."

She walks to the door with the plate in her hand. "Yeah, I guess I'll see you around."

You won't. That was it. And believe me you're better off. As I close the door, the only thing I feel is relief that I won't have to go to the grocery store until tomorrow.

Chapter Four

"Mack Marsh, you make her wear that hat! The sun is turning her hair as red as an apple!" Camille yelled as Mack and Millie walked down the porch stairs hand-in-hand. She knew he wouldn't listen to her. He never did anymore.

Camille turned back to Beatrice who was fanning herself vigorously with the magazine she found next to her lawn chair on the front porch. Even in the morning, July was already showing its ugly side.

"I always said if my child had red hair, I'd drown it in a lake," Camille said, pouring herself another glass of lemonade as she settled back into her chair.

"Well technically, you don't have a child with red hair. She's Mack's daughter," Beatrice said, pressing her cold glass against her temple. She wanted to remind Camille that Mack had bright red hair when he was born.

Camille knew what Beatrice was thinking. "Mack's red hair all but disappeared when he was five."

"Because you dyed it," Beatrice said. "You probably burned every brain cell in that poor boy's head. Putting that dye on a baby."

"I did not dye his hair, Beatrice Tucker. It just got darker as he got older." And, she'd been relieved when it did. Camille didn't want any memory of Mack's father around.

Beatrice sighed. She'd given up trying to resurrect the Camille she once knew. That carefree spirit had disappeared the day Camille got pregnant.

"Well, Millie's hair is getting blonder and blonder. Maybe all that strawberry will go away eventually," said Beatrice.

Mack shook his head as their voices died away. He didn't know how Beatrice had dealt with his mother all these years. She'd been the only one to stick around after Camille got pregnant. Beatrice told Mack everything when he was growing up. Everything. Things he didn't really want to know about his mom, especially that he had been conceived in a one-night stand. But really, as uncomfortable as it was to think about, he always believed it was better to know. It helped explain Camille's negative outlook on life, at least a little bit.

As they rounded the last corner to the beach, Millie started dancing and spinning like she did every time she saw the ocean. They'd made this walk at least a hundred times, but she always acted like she was seeing the water for the first time. Millie insisted, as always, that they immediately get in the ocean. Mack had her in the water by the time she was six months old. She took to it immediately, just like he had. He picked her up, took her past the break into waist-deep water, and held her as she bobbed up and down.

"Daddy, I want to swim like you do. Let go of me, please," Millie said impatiently.

She had already developed the courage and confidence of someone well beyond her three years. Not to mention the language skills. She started talking in complex sentences when she was just two.

"Sweetie, we're in the ocean. It's dangerous. Daddy has to hang on to you for now. But when you're older, you'll be able to swim like a fish just like me."

"Daddy, you're not a fish—you're a seal!" Millie let out a peal of laughter that echoed off the waves.

The words made Mack jump. "Who told you I was a SEAL, Millie?"

"Camille said that you're a seal, and you kill people, but that's silly because seals can't kill people," she said definitively.

Mack breathed in sharply. He'd told Camille not to discuss his work with Millie or anyone else for that matter. But especially Millie. He knew it didn't mean anything to her at this age, but as she grew up, he didn't want her to know how dangerous his job was.

"Daddy, throw me, throw me!" Millie was kicking her legs in the surf ferociously, trying to propel her body into the air.

Mack flung Millie in the air and watched her splash down a few feet from him. She quickly surfaced and paddled her way back over to him. He caught her just before the wave hit, protecting her from the break with his body.

After almost an hour of doing this, he finally convinced her to come out of the water. Mack rolled her up like a burrito in an oversized beach towel, leaving only her head visible, just like she liked it. She laid in the sand—her head on his lap—and was asleep in minutes.

Mack had reenlisted in the navy for a couple more years, but he spent every second of his downtime in the Outer Banks with Millie. Camille agreed to keep her as long as he needed, especially after he told her he would get a raise for re-upping, and that she would be getting half of that, too. Mack knew he should quit and be with Millie full time, but he couldn't bring himself to do it. The teams had such a strong hold on him.

Millie was his family, but his team was his family, too. He thought he had figured out a way to manage both families. He just hoped it was the right thing for Millie. She seemed happy and well-adjusted. In reality, he saw her almost as much as the other guys saw their kids. Camille's house was only an hour drive from the base. He drove down there every time he had a break, even if it was only for a few hours.

Most importantly, he knew Millie was much less visible in the Outer Banks than she would be in Virginia Beach. After more than three years, he had started to think they weren't even looking for her.

Mack wasn't sure how long he had been lost in his thoughts when he heard Millie's sleepy voice. "Daddy, I just had a dream about Mommy. She's in heaven."

"Yeah, sweetie, she is. She looks down on you every day. She loves you so much." He always tried to distract her when she thought about her mom. He wasn't ready to have that conversation yet. "Hey, is it time for us to have ice cream? I'm getting hungry."

"Yes!" Millie was suddenly up and spinning around in the sand. "I want strawberry!"

"I know you want strawberry," Mack said, picking her up and throwing her over his shoulder. "It's all you ever eat. You're going to turn into a giant strawberry."

As they got close to the ice cream shop, Mack saw a girl a little older than Millie running toward them at breakneck speed.

"Millie!" she screamed. The two girls collided with an ear-splitting series of squeals.

"You must be Millie's dad." Mack turned to find a woman staring at him.

"Yeah, Mack Marsh," he said, extending his hand. "I'm guessing you belong to the other one."

"I'm Carol Blake, Chloe's mom. Would you like to share our table?" She pointed over toward the corner. Mack didn't really want to, but Millie and Chloe were already over there whispering aggressively to each other.

"Sure, that's nice. Thanks. Let me grab her a cone."

He came out to find Millie and Chloe playing in a nearby fountain.

"I hope you don't mind," Carol said. "It's just so hot out today."

"No worries. We just got back from the beach. She's already in need of about a hundred baths."

Millie's cone began to melt on his hand, so he started licking.

"You've got a little in your beard," Carol said, pointing.

"Yeah, it's one of the hazards of having a beard," he said, trying to wipe the ice cream out with his hand.

"Camille tells me you're a SEAL."

23

Mack's mind snapped back to the conversation he was going to have with Camille. It wasn't going to be pretty.

"You know Camille, huh?" he said, ignoring her comment.

"Does anyone not know Camille?"

Mack rolled his eyes and smiled a little bit again. "Yeah, my mom has never really been shy."

Millie and Chloe had made it back over to the table.

"Daddy, you ate all the fluffy ice cream top," Millie said, her lips pouting.

"It was melting, sweetie. I'll buy you a new one," Mack said as he stood up. "We should really be getting back home. I need to head back to the base tonight."

Carol looked disappointed. "Why don't I give you my number if you need anything while you're away? Millie and Chloe are really close. I'd be happy to keep in touch with you."

Mack typed her number into his phone. "Say goodbye, Millie. We need to go."

Mack bought Millie another cone which she declared very dramatically she was too tired to eat after only two licks. So Mack downed another strawberry cone as he carried her sleepy body in his other arm.

Mack barely got her out of the bath before she was fast asleep. He tucked her in and headed back downstairs. Camille was just finishing her lunch.

"There's some left if you want any before you leave," she said in his general direction.

Mack walked up behind her and pulled her chair out swiftly from the table. He leaned down until his face was even with hers. "If you ever talk to Millie or anyone else about my job again, I swear I'll kill you while you sleep. Do you understand me?"

Camille nodded immediately. She had never seen his eyes look that deadly or heard such a frightening tone in his voice.

"I have to head back to the base. I'll be back in a few days," he said as he walked away. "If that child isn't the happiest she's ever been when I get back, we will have a problem."

Camille didn't move until she heard his car pulling out of the driveway.

Chapter Five

"My God, Millie. It's just Monday. Can't you give me a few days to get into the week before you dump shit like this on me?" George has been my boss since my first day in the agency, and despite his perpetual irritability, he's one of the kindest people I know.

"He's alive, George. I know he is. I've been tracking him since the day I started here." I watch him shift uncomfortably in his chair.

"On your own. Not at my direction."

I can tell he's feeling emasculated, and I know I have to tread lightly.

"I should have told you about it sooner, but I wanted to make sure I had something."

George stops shifting. It's never taken much contrition from me to win him over to my side.

"Millie, I want to help you, but everyone's going to think I'm crazy if I try to push this through. The agency has been chasing Sayid Custovic for decades. Everyone has all but given up. He hasn't been seen in almost twenty years. He's dead. He has to be."

"Then how do you explain his organization still surviving? Even thriving?"

"Those organizations are like weeds. You know that. You kill one leader, and another one pops up in his place. You know as well as I do that Yusef Hadzic runs that network now," he says.

"Well, then let me go after Hadzic."

"Millie, you've barely been here for three years. And I know you've had a meteoric rise, but you're still too green to say 'I'm the one to get Yusef Hadzic.' We've been trying to get him for years. Agents with a lot more experience have tried and failed."

"I found a new lead."

George starts shifting again. "What new lead?"

"I found Amar Petrovic, Custovic's best friend growing up."

"I've never heard of him."

"No one has. His family moved to Spain after the war. He's just recently moved back to Sarajevo."

"How do you know he even knew Custovic?" George shifts again.

"They lived right next door to each other from the time they were born until the war basically wiped out their neighborhood. I have real estate records, school records. Their fathers were both leaders at the same mosque. They were friends. I know they were."

"So they were childhood friends—it doesn't mean they

kept in touch. Custovic radicalized after the war. This Amar guy moved to Spain. They probably lost touch."

"I thought that, too, but since I located Petrovic back in Sarajevo, I've had our agents there tracking him."

"You've done what? Millie, you can't make field assignments. Who approved this?" He already knows no one did, so I ignore the question.

"It wasn't anything formal. I worked on an interrogation with one of the agents over there last year. We've kept in touch. She's doing me a favor."

"God, Millie, you can't just do this shit. You have to work through the proper channels."

"Do you want to hear what she found or not?"

George sighs deeply. "I know you're going to tell me, regardless of what I want, so go ahead."

"She's been trailing Petrovic for four months."

"Four months? Millie." George stops shifting and puts his face in his hands.

"Yes, four months. And in that time, she's observed random men—always different men—handing Petrovic burner phones. They stop him on the street, hand him the phone, and walk away. The phone rings almost immediately. Petrovic talks on the phone for about five minutes, and then throws it away. This has happened at least nine times in the past four months."

George looks up at me, grimacing. "Yeah, I mean, that's suspicious, but he could be a drug runner. Maybe it's his mistress. None of that proves he's talking to Custovic. Has the agent gotten close enough to hear the conversations?"

"No, but she's picked up most of the phones. She's pinged the numbers that call him. They always hit in the Afghanistan mountains. Different areas, but always up near the Hindu Kush. That's where Custovic set up shop after the war."

George sits up straight. I know I have him now.

"George, there's no one in those tribal areas except the true believers. Even if he's not talking to Custovic, he's up to something. Maybe it's the reason he moved back to Bosnia after twenty years. It's something. And I think it's something big."

George thinks for a few minutes. I can almost see the wheels turning in his head.

"I still don't believe Custovic is alive, but I do agree that Petrovic's behavior is suspicious. It wouldn't hurt for us to pick him up and question him," he says slowly, wheels still spinning. "I'll make this happen for you on one condition: that you don't mention Sayid Custovic's name to anyone. This is just an op to pick up Petrovic and find out what he's up to."

"Agreed."

"I'll set the wheels in motion for a SEAL team to pick him up. You'll need to go down to Virginia Beach to brief them."

Just the mention of Virginia Beach makes me want to throw up. In the eight years since my dad died, I've learned to steel myself by burying my emotions. I haven't let them get close to the surface in years, but thinking about going back to Virginia Beach is sending shockwaves through my body. I have to keep the emotions buried, but I can feel them getting stronger, just waiting for the most inopportune time to explode.

"Do I have to work with a SEAL team?" I say cautiously.

"Why? Do you just want to grab Petrovic by yourself?" George says sarcastically, but I know he's more than half worried I might think that's a possibility.

"I know I can't get him myself, George. It's just. . . you know what I mean." George is one of the only people in the agency—in my life—that knows my dad was a SEAL, and that he died on a mission.

"Millie, your dad was one of them. You, of all people, should know what these guys do, and how well they do it."

"He never really talked to me about what he did. I was totally separate from that part of his life. Until . . ." My eyes start welling up. Damn it. I look at my feet. You'd think after eight years, it would get easier. But it never does.

"Until he was killed?" George says softly.

"Yeah. That was the first time I'd ever been around any of them. And I didn't want to be around them. I wanted to forget everything about what they did to him."

"Millie, they didn't do anything to him. At most, they kept him alive way longer than he probably should have lived. These guys don't exactly have long life expectancies."

"Just going back there," I say, pausing to try to stop the tear that wants to escape my left eye. "Did I ever tell you Virginia Beach was the last place I saw him? At that base."

George squints which he only does when he's getting concerned. I straighten up quickly. I don't want him to send someone else to do this. It has to be me. There is no other choice. If this is going to end the way I think it's going to end, it has to be me.

"Do you want me to have Raine take this one? She already

works with the teams."

"No, definitely not," I say quickly. "This is my op."

"Look, I know how strong you are, Millie. You're a rock. It will be hard to be back there, but just go in, do your job, and get back to D.C. where you belong."

I knew I didn't have any other choice.

"Agreed."

"And again, no talking to them or anyone about Custovic. This is just an op for Petrovic."

I nod and start to walk out.

"Oh and, Millie, you're still a pain in my ass. I haven't told you that recently, but I want to make sure you know your status hasn't changed."

"Agreed," I say, smiling at him as I close his office door.

It's already well after nine by the time we end our meeting. I decide to head home for the night. I'm barely back in my apartment when I get a text from George.

You're expected in Virginia Beach on Wednesday morning for an 8am briefing. Contact Captain Harrison Culver of DEVGRU. He's a friend... Be at least 15 minutes early. Probably 30 minutes to be safe. These guys are a different sort... Let me know how it goes. Good luck.

I try to get some sleep, but it's worthless. It's three in the morning, and I'm wide awake. I wasn't planning on going down there until tonight, but I know I'm not going to get anything done until I rip off the bandage.

As soon as I see the exit signs for Virginia Beach, the tears start streaming down my face, slowly at first, and then so forcefully I have to pull over. I thought I could do this by myself, but I know now that I need backup. I text Raine.

Just pulled into VB. You up for a coffee?

She texts back in record speed, especially for her.

Millie Vanilli!!! I thought you were coming in tonight?? Yes, coffee. Meet me at the Starbucks near Neptune's Park. I'll be there in 10.

I have absolutely no idea where that is. I only lived here a few months after Dad died and, for most of that time, I was lying in bed, trying to remember that breathing happened naturally.

"You got lost didn't you?" Raine is standing by her car in front of Starbucks, waiting for me.

"You know I've always been directionally challenged."

"No wonder you don't work in the field much," she says, coming over to hug me. "Girl, I've missed you. I'm so glad you're going to be here for a few weeks."

Raine and I met in training at Langley. She was really the only one of my classmates that I liked, and vice versa, so we were pretty much inseparable for the better part of a year.

We get our lattes and sit down. I take off my sunglasses and realize the mistake I've made much too late.

"What the fuck? Oh my God, Millie, your eyes are so red and puffy," she says. "I knew this was going to be too much for you."

I put my sunglasses back on quickly, hoping she'll forget what she's just seen. No such luck.

"Really, Mills? Are you just going to wear sunglasses the entire time you're here?"

I take them off again. "I just sat in my car on the side of the highway for almost thirty minutes, trying to decide if I could do this. I decided I could, and I'm going to, but I need today to work through this before my meetings tomorrow."

"One day, huh? All your repressed emotions are going to disappear in a day?"

"They're not going to disappear, Raine, but I can keep them under control," I say, not sure if I believe it myself. "I promise."

"Well, I'm definitely not going to let you do this alone. I can come with you."

"I thought you were on an assignment with another team."

"I am, but this team you're going to work with. . . I mean, they're probably the best assault team in the squad, but they're a lot to deal with. I'm not sure your first outing with them should be alone, especially with all this happening," she says, gesturing to my eyes.

"I'll be fine. Really. I needed to have a good cry. I've had one. I'm just ready to get on with it," I say. "Tell me about the team. I've read their files, but give me your read."

"I mean they're all alpha males. Don't really like bullshit. Straight shooters, literally and figuratively. They don't really talk that much, you know. Just be honest, give them good information, and let them do their jobs. They're the best at it."

"Tell me more about them individually," I say, draining the last of my latte.

"Well, Mason Davis is the team leader. He's really solid. Tough, smart. Bullheaded. Can be a total asshole, but he's right about almost everything. And he's successful. Rarely fails at a mission."

She pauses to look at a text. I look at mine, too. Another text from Chase. I never responded to him over the weekend.

Millie. Call me. Right now. I know what you're doing. Stop it. Now.

Raine starts up again. "Then there's the second in command, Julius Jackson. Everyone calls him JJ. Absolutely no personality. He's the size of a mountain. I mean, he's totally jacked. I don't know how he moves as fast as he does. He's one of the trained snipers on the team. Just fucking intimidating from start to finish."

It's funny to hear her talk about these guys. It reminds me of how my friends reacted to my dad the first time they met him. It was always the same: they were scared of him until they figured out what a complete teddy bear he was underneath all of the bravado.

"Butch Harrison. Short, compact, all mouth. Georgia redneck. Tough as nails. But just always talking. Ty Miller. Quiet, always observing, probably knows everything about everything. He's the most highly trained medic on the team."

"How many medics do they have on each team?" I ask.

"I mean they're all trained at field medical. One of them is almost always dinged somehow on a mission, so they all need to have the basic skills. Only a few are trained to do critical care in the field though."

I guess there was no one trained to help my dad when the house he was clearing blew up all around him.

"Do they know about your dad?" Raine seems to be reading my mind.

"What? No. No one knows except the higher-ups at the agency and you."

"You should tell them, Millie. They take the family thing really seriously here. Your dad was one of them. It makes you one of them."

"I'm not part of it. I told you Dad kept me away from all this. I only met a few of them after he died."

"It doesn't matter. They'll want to know. It's something you should tell them. Really."

"I don't want them to know. I don't want anyone to know. You can't tell them."

"You know I won't," she says.

I do know she won't. She's the most solid friend I've ever had.

"Is that the entire team?"

"No, they usually run with six or seven on a team. Let me see, who haven't I told you about? Um, Mitch Davidson. They call him Mouse because he's really small next to the other guys. Crazy fast. By far the best swimmer on the team. Bryce Barton, new guy on the team, just out of sniper school. Seems solid. And Hawk Fuller, whose God-given name is really Hawk. He's a knuckle dragger. You know, the guy who will do the dirty work. And, he's really good at it. Probably wouldn't want to do anything else."

"Well, they sound like a really fun group of guys to be around," I say, laughing.

"They're all right." She rolls her eyes. "And, they're going to loooooove you."

"Meaning?"

"You still look like a fucking Barbie doll, Millie. I thought George was trying to make you blend in a bit more."

"He was, but as it turns out, this look works surprisingly well in interrogations."

"What does that mean?"

"You know most of the guys I interrogate are the religious zealots. They like women to shut up, cover up, and disappear into the woodwork. When I walk into the room, I think it kind of freaks them out."

"Shit, I've been called a whore so many times, I can't imagine how many times you have."

"Um, fuck you," I say, smiling.

"No, I mean, look at you—the hair, the skin, the eyes, the body, and especially the attitude. You have to be their worst nightmare."

"One guy told me I looked like a ghost," I say, smiling proudly.

"That's hilarious. I bet he gave it up pretty quickly."

"Well, he definitely didn't like being in the room alone with me."

Raine's phone is blowing up. "Mills, I'm sorry. I have to go. Do you want to meet for a drink tonight? I can probably introduce you to the team. They usually hang out at a bar by the base on Tuesday nights. Dollar pitchers and free pool tables. They rarely miss it when they're in town. Might be a good idea to meet them socially before the work starts."

"Yeah, that sounds good. Text me later."

As I watch her walk away, it occurs to me that this might be one of the last times I'll ever see her. I've known all along that I'll probably end up dead at the end of this. I'm fine with that if it means finding out the truth. But it's just now that I'm realizing what it might do to the handful of people in my life who love me, including Chase.

Chapter Six

MASON, VIRGINIA BEACH, VIRGINIA, 2019

"I swear to God if I don't get to shoot someone pretty soon, I will lose my goddamn mind," Butch says as he empties yet another practice round down-range.

"Yeah, I don't think your goal should be shooting people, and from what I can tell, your mind's been gone for years," Ty says.

"Oh yeah, now you're going to talk. You don't say anything for days at a time, but today you have an opinion." Butch ejects the empty mag from his pistol and sighs as he walks away.

We just completed another day of training, and we're all getting twitchy. Believe me, the last thing you want operators to be is twitchy. We haven't been out on a mission in almost a month. It's fucking annoying. It's like an athlete training every day, but never getting on the field. I just want to get an op or, better yet, get back on deployment. I'm in the worst mood I've been in for a while and, believe me, that's saying something.

"Mason, I need to talk to you before you leave tonight." I turn around to see Culver standing next to our ready room.

"You got something for us?" I ask hopefully.

"Yeah, maybe. Not sure about it yet. Stop by my office on the way out."

Culver is an old SEAL, a captain now. He's the head of our unit. Decent guy. Smart. Wound as tight as a top though. I really don't want to end my day with any more bullshit.

The guys are headed out to the bar. Again. Like every night. It's where we spend the most time besides the base. I tell them I'll meet them there with no intention of showing up. All I want to do is go home and sulk on my couch. I've been doing that a lot lately. It's the only thing I have the energy to do. Being inactive makes me tired. Way more tired than going hard for weeks on end. When we're working, my adrenaline surges. When we're home, it dies away. It's on life support right now.

I knock on Culver's door as I walk in. "So what's the new op?"

"We have a new agent coming in tomorrow morning to brief us on it. It's some kind of snatch-and-grab in Sarajevo."

"Sarajevo? That hasn't been active for years."

"Yeah, I'm not sure what it's all about. Friend of mine at the agency calling in a favor. They think the guy is somehow tied to radicals in Afghanistan. Maybe even part of the Hadzic Network."

"Yusef Hadzic? Haven't we tried to go after him about twenty times?" I've been on two missions to grab him that ended up being dry holes. I'm not even sure he's still alive."

"Yeah, I know. Again, not a hundred percent sure. We'll find out tomorrow," he says.

"Who's the new spook? They replacing Raine?" I hope they aren't. Raine's pretty solid. And, most importantly, she's been easy to train.

"No. This is just a one-time thing. She's been tracking this guy. Has all of the intel. She'll work with Raine," Culver says. I'm noticing something weird about the way he's talking about her. I can't put my finger on what it is yet.

"You ask Raine about her?"

"Yeah. Apparently, she's a rising star in D.C. Mainly an interrogator, but supposedly a very effective one. Broken some big targets, especially for her age. She's just in her mid-twenties."

"She ever worked outside of D.C.?"

In general, I hate everyone from D.C. They usually bring a lot of red-tape bullshit with them. I'm not a very patient person.

"Yeah, she's been in-country extensively, but never attached to one of our teams. I think she comes in after the HVT is in-house. Here's her file." He pushes it across the desk.

I flip the file open and review it quickly. I'm not all that interested if she's just going to be with us for one mission. Millie Marsh. Age 25. NYU and George Washington graduate. Fluent in Bosnian, Spanish, Pashto. Semi-fluent in Farsi and Bari. Fine. Whatever. Sounds like an average agent.

I leave Culver's office more frustrated than when I went in. I didn't join the teams to sit on my ass, and I definitely didn't join them to go after some soft target in Bosnia. The teams have been nonstop for almost two decades. The War on Terror has kept us busy, but it's slowing down now. I'm not saying that's a bad thing, but it's frustrating. I feel like fifteen years of my life are coming to a crashing halt.

Our next deployment is still a month away, and I can't wait for it to get here. When I'm home, I have too much time to think. Thinking is a bad thing. I need distraction, and I need it quickly. My non-military friends, all two of them, think I'm crazy when I tell them I want to be in Iraq or Afghanistan for three or four months at a time. And they're not wrong. I mean, it's not exactly fun.

The best way I can describe it is, you know that vacation feeling? The night before you leave, you're all hyped up, can't wait to get there. And then the first few days are great, just how you imagined. But by like day four, you realize you've gone too hard—you're hungover, sunburned, and all your clothes are dirty, so you start thinking that going back home won't be so bad. Then, you get home, you wash your clothes, your sunburn fades, and all you want to do is go back on vacation.

That's how deployment has always felt for me. Can't wait to get there to do the job I fucking love. After a few weeks of it, I'm exhausted and dirty, and can't wait to get back home. After being back home for a few days, I'm bored and twitchy, and can't wait to get back on deployment. It's a vicious cycle.

My family doesn't understand my life choices either. My brother followed my dad into the family business. They run a liquor wholesaler in Houston. I probably would have done that, too, but when my mom died when I was ten, my life turned upside down.

I remember my dad showing me a dilapidated house in our neighborhood when I was about that age. He told me to stay away from it. That the guy living there had been injured in the Vietnam War, and was a little crazy. As I got toward my teenage years, I started resenting my dad and doing the opposite of whatever he asked of me. So the perfect rebellion was to visit the crazy man's house.

I went over there when I was twelve or thirteen. Just walked right up to his door and knocked. I was already almost six feet tall by that age. I wasn't afraid of much. Frank answered the door with a beer in his hand. It was ten in the morning. He asked me if I wanted one. I said yes, mostly out of confusion. We sat on his front porch and drank our beers, and he started telling me about being in the navy, and about being one of the first-ever SEALs.

From the second he started talking, I knew what I wanted to do with my life. He didn't make it sound romantic. In fact, he made it sound like hell. But I saw the way his face lit up when he talked about his team, his brothers. I knew I wanted that. Against my dad's wishes, I joined the navy right out of high school. I got my trident by the time I was twenty. That makes it sound easy. It wasn't. It was hell. But it was perfect hell—dirty, exhausting, painful. Everything Frank told me it was going to be.

I'm thinking about all this on my way home and it's not sitting well. I do a U-turn toward the bar. All the guys are there already when I walk in. Pete has my whiskey ready by the time I walk by the bar. I join the rest of my team over by the pool table. They're all jawing at each other about something. More of the same.

I sit on a stool drinking, looking around at tonight's offerings. They're everywhere. The Frog Hogs. That's what we call them. The girls that come to the bar just for us. It's not a very flattering nickname, but believe me, they earn it every night. They're all carefully orbiting the pool table, not having the nerve to walk over and start talking, but making sure we see them when we're ready. I don't see anything worthwhile, so I just keep drinking. Eventually, that will make the offerings start to look better.

I'm about four whiskeys in by the time Butch and I finish off our last victims. No one beats us at pool, and we never let anyone break up our team. Why mess with perfection? Butch is trying to convince someone to lose another hundred to us. As usual, I let him do the talking. It's what he does best. As I'm sitting back on my stool, something at the door catches my eye. And that's when I see her. For the first time in weeks, my adrenaline starts surging.

Chapter Seven

"I don't know how many times I have to tell you to stay away from those lilac bushes, Millicent. They're just thick with bees this time of year," Camille said as she clamped down on Millie's arm, now red and swelling from bee stings.

Camille was frustrated by everything about this child. Millie was trusting, optimistic, and silly—the exact opposite of her. Camille had tried from day one to discourage those qualities in Millie, but they just kept popping back up like the short-lived weeds in Camille's meticulous garden.

"I was just trying to get them to sit on my arm like the butterflies do," Millie said insistently.

Millie played in the yard for hours, talking to any friend she could find—birds, squirrels, butterflies. Camille told Mack she thought the child was half simple but, as usual, Mack encouraged Millie's behavior. It drove Camille crazy that Mack wasn't raising Millie to recognize the harsh realities of the world. Camille looked forward to when Mack was on deployment for three or four months at a time. That gave her the opportunity to really work on correcting some of Millie's more annoying behaviors. But then Mack would always come back, and the two of them would ruin all the hard work Camille had put in.

"Sit still, Millicent." Camille pushed Millie down on the lawn chair as she tried for the third time to apply the baking soda paste to the stings.

"Let the paste dry before you get up," Camille said as she turned swiftly to go back into the house, the screen door slamming definitively behind her.

Millie laid back on the lawn chair and closed her eyes. She hated when Camille called her Millicent. It was her given name, but she thought it sounded mean, especially the way Camille said it. She liked the name Millie. That's what her daddy called her. The chair's polyester straps were digging uncomfortably into her bare legs, but she didn't dare move. She knew Camille was watching from the kitchen, waiting for another reason to scold her.

I'll just wait here for Daddy, she thought. Millie heard Camille on the phone with him last night. As usual, Camille told him he didn't need to come, but Millie knew he'd show up. He always did.

Mack didn't bother going into the house when he arrived. He had to be back in Virginia Beach in a few hours. He didn't want to waste any of his time on Camille's nonsense. He found Millie on the porch sleeping uncomfortably on a lawn chair. Her little arms had turned as red as the persistent strawberry streaks in her golden hair.

"Millie, sweetie." He shook her gently.

"Daddy!" She leaped out of the chair and into his arms.

Mack carried her to the shade of the overgrown oak tree in the front yard. He tried to put her down on the grass, but she maneuvered herself until she was sitting on his lap. She rested her head against his broad chest and, as usual, his heart melted.

"Sweetie, you can't fall asleep in the sun. You're getting a sunburn and little blisters," Mack said, running his big, calloused hands lightly over her little arms.

"Oh no Daddy, that's not a sunburn. The bees bit me."

"Oh, sweetie, do they hurt?" Mack lightly kissed them, making her giggle. Mack wanted to record that sound and take it with him everywhere he went.

"Were you under the lilacs again?" He already knew the answer. That was her favorite place in the yard.

She shrugged and nuzzled in closer to his chest. He never got mad at her like Camille did, but she liked to make sure. She knew her daddy liked to snuggle.

"Sweetie, you have to stay away from those bushes in the summer. I told you that last time."

She sighed like the weight of the world rested on her little shoulders. "Why are the bees so mean to me? I want them to like me. The butterflies like me."

"Millie, bees aren't like butterflies. They're workers. They have a job to do, and that's all they want to do. They don't have time to sit on your arms."

"They can take a break like everyone else does," Millie said.

The world is so simple to her, Mack thought. And that's the way he wanted to keep it.

"They don't want breaks, sweetie. They like their work, and they just want to do nothing but that. If you try to get in their way, you get stung." Mack smiled as he realized he was basically describing himself.

"Everybody likes breaks," Millie said, sighing dramatically at such a crazy notion.

"Bees don't. It's just the way they're built. God made them that way. It's not right or wrong. It's just how they are."

"Butterflies take breaks. They don't work."

"Well, they do some work, but they don't work very hard. They just fly around from flower to flower and only work when they want to. They don't really have a plan. Butterflies just land on whatever flower looks nice to them and makes them happy."

Millie sighed as she let the hot summer breeze begin to lull her back to sleep. "Daddy, I'd really rather be a butterfly."

"You are, sweetie. You're a butterfly," he said as he gently stroked her hair. He couldn't imagine how she was going to survive in the world, but he loved her spirit and encouraged her to be carefree—something he hadn't felt one day during his childhood.

Mack knew Camille wasn't a good influence on her. He thought several times about moving Millie to Virginia Beach, and hiring a nanny when he worked. But he knew he'd just be trading one evil for another, and shockingly, Camille was the lesser of the evils. Mack didn't want Millie anywhere near his professional life. When he was in Virginia Beach, he ate, slept, and breathed his job. The minute he crossed over the Virginia-North Carolina border on his way to see Millie, he transformed into a different person. He needed to keep that separation for his sake, as much as hers.

Unless he had a career-ending injury, Mack figured he had about ten years left of being an operator. He could retire with full pension before he was forty. He planned to move with Millie somewhere near the naval base in San Diego, maybe teach a few classes to new recruits. Millie could go to college in California, and they'd go surfing in her free time. He had it all figured out. Now, he just had to get there.

Chapter Eight

Mills, I'm still slammed at work. Can't meet you at the bar.
Sorry. See you tomorrow. Don't be late. They're freaky about
punctuality.

I've been staring at Raine's text in the bar's parking lot for
about five minutes. I can't decide if I should go in without her
or not. I'm not in the most social mood, but I need a change of
scenery from the hotel room, and I could really use a drink.
What the hell. Let's do this.

The bar's already in full swing by the time I walk in. I
notice immediately that I don't look much like the rest of the
women in here. They're wearing the ultimate bar-battle gear:
micro-short dresses, full makeup, dazzling manicures, and hair
that has been curled and sprayed to perfection. Honestly, I'm a
little jealous. Even if I wanted to look like that, I wouldn't
know where to begin. I grew up at the beach. Being in and out

of the water that much didn't lend itself to makeup, managed hair, or manicures.

I stand at the bar's door and watch them for a second, the coiffed ladies perched on their barstools, ready to pounce if any man looks their way. Most of their flirtatious smiles and longing gazes seem to be fixed on one place: the pool tables. I look over there to see my new SEAL team holding court.

I don't recognize them immediately. They don't look much like the official navy pictures in their files, but it's them. If there was a central casting call for operators, they definitely would fit the bill—scraggly beards, long hair, lean, compact, muscular, tattoos, scars. They remind me of my dad for a second, and that sends an intense shot of pain down my body. I definitely need a drink.

I'm trying to get the bartender's attention. Apparently, his name is Pete and boy, let me tell you, Pete is not having a good time. There's a gaggle of drunk girls just to the left of me screeching at him for another round. I feel you, man. They annoy me, too. Finally, Pete makes his way over to me. He just stares at me. I don't think he likes newcomers.

"Dirty martini, please," I say, sincerely hoping it's okay for me to talk. I'm really not sure from the way he's looking at me.

"I don't make martinis, and I have no idea what a dirty one is."

"Just add some olive juice into the martini . . ." It's just registering with me that he said he didn't make martinis. He's glaring at me.

"How about a Maker's on the rocks?" I ask quickly.

"I have Wild Turkey," he says as he turns around and starts

making my drink without asking me if Wild Turkey is okay. It's not, but I'm sure as hell not telling Pete that.

I turn my stool around to view the pool game. Mason Davis is staring at me. Maybe he's already figured out who I am. Raine told me he's quick. I have to say his official navy picture doesn't do him justice. He's clean cut in the picture— looking pretty average—but tonight he looks gruff, and intense, and just really, really sexy.

His file says he's thirty-five, but he looks at least five years older. His skin looks weathered, which I remember from my dad is a side effect of the job. He has sandy blond curls coming out the sides of his baseball cap. He looks like he hasn't shaved in at least a month. His beard's getting scraggly, with wisps of gray hair shooting out here and there.

The file lists him as six feet, 210 pounds, but he looks a lot leaner than that. His T-shirt is baggy and untucked, but it's not doing a thing to hide his absolutely chiseled arms. I notice what looks like the tip of a trident tattoo coming out of his right sleeve. It probably starts on his shoulder. I'd really like to explore this theory further.

He's not saying much, but all eyes are on him—men and women. He's definitely the center of attention. I'm watching as he lifts the front of his shirt to wipe something off his face. I just see the ripped stomach muscles that wind down and disappear into his jeans before he puts the shirt back down.

He looks up at me again and smiles confidently. He knows the effect he has on women. He's so arrogant that it makes me feel a little light-headed. I cross my legs to keep from falling off the stool. I smile and look away quickly just in case he's staring for other reasons. I don't want to encourage him. This is strictly business. But damn, he's not like anything I've seen in D.C.

Pete finally makes it over with my drink. I down it before he can walk away, and motion for another. He nods. I think sign language is going to be my best bet with Pete. I swivel back around to watch the pool game. It looks like Mason is partnered with Butch. They're just putting the finishing touches on this game. Butch is talking all kinds of smack with a deep Southern drawl. He's looking for their next victims and waving around a hundred dollar bill—daring anyone to challenge them. Well, I guess there's no time like the present to meet the team. I might as well put to use some of the skills I learned in college.

"I'll play," I say as I slide off the bar stool, and walk over to them.

They all stop in their tracks—none of them trying to conceal the once-over they're giving me. In Mason's case, it's two or three times over, and it's definitely making me sweat.

Finally, Butch speaks up. "You'll play with us? Not sure you know what you're getting into, ma'am?"

Oh, sweetie, I so do. I know everything about you and your friends. And what I know about all men is they're rarely paying enough attention to know they're getting hustled until it's already way too late.

Chapter Nine

I see her the minute she walks in. She opens the door and it's like someone shines a flashlight into my eyes. Her long, blonde hair is glowing through the haze of the bar. She's tall and slender, and from what I can make out from this distance, her legs start somewhere up around her chest. I immediately think about how they would feel wrapped all around me.

She starts maneuvering her way expertly through the drunk men. They're leering at her. It makes me want to pull out my rifle, and shoot a round of warning shots over their heads. I watch as they brush up against her on purpose. She deftly changes direction every time it happens, ignoring their filthy eyes and hungry greetings. There's no doubt in my mind this happens every time she walks into a room.

She's only about twenty feet from me now. I get a better look at her. She looks like she just came off the beach—cutoffs, T-shirt, flip flops. Her skin and hair both still radiate the sun's glow. She takes a stool at the bar with her back toward me. Her hair sways back and forth as she settles into her seat. I'm hypnotized by it. I want to dip my hands deep into it, and feel it flow over me like water.

I hear her saying something to Pete. It sounds like she's ordered something other than beer or whiskey. That's really where his bartending skills start and end. Pete leaves to get her a drink that I'm sure is going to be nothing like what she ordered. She turns her stool around and looks right at me. She sees me looking. I don't try to hide it. She smiles slightly to acknowledge, but not to encourage, and looks away. The disappointment shoots all the way through my body.

I've seen her type before. Not often. Certainly not in this town. A woman like her is like a mirage—an illusion sent to trick you into thinking something on the horizon could actually quench your thirst. But in the back of your head, you know it's not real. You're never even going to be able to get close to it.

I don't look away though. I'm not sure I physically can. My eyes dart up and down her body not sure where they want to land. There's so much to look at. I'm enjoying the subtle curves peeking out of her loose V-neck T-shirt when she crosses her legs, drawing my eyes slowly, all the way down her long, long legs. As I'm thinking about how I'd like to start at her ankles and run my hands all the way up until they disappear under her shorts, I notice suddenly that the legs have started walking toward me.

"I'll play," she says to us, to me, to the team.

Seeing what we see every day, it takes a lot to bring us to a complete stop. But here we are, seven grizzled operators stopped in our tracks—leering thirstily at the mirage.

Butch is the first to recover. "You'll play with us? Not sure you know what you're getting into, ma'am." He extends out the word "ma'am" to highlight his Southern drawl. It's one of his go-to pickup moves.

"Oh, I think I probably do." She doesn't look too concerned.

"We're like professional pool players, darlin'," Butch continues. "You ought not to mess with us."

"I'll take my chances, but I get to pick my partner."

I watch as my team suddenly straightens up like they're in the operator version of a beauty pageant, pumping out their chests and trying to smooth their beards.

"I want curly back there." She points at Mouse. As usual, he's the only one not seeking the spotlight. Currently, he's trying to blend into the wall.

"Mouse? All this on display, and you want that?" Butch is flexing so hard, I think he might pop a bicep.

"Women are always suckers for the strong, silent type. Am I right?" she says turning to Clark, one of the naval analysts assigned to our team. Clark rolls her eyes. She's about as interested in us as we are in her.

"Well, she's not going to say anything because she knows y'all, but trust me, she looks at those curls," the mirage says, nodding toward Mouse, who's about to keel over from all the attention being leveled at him.

She smiles, picks up a cue, and walks past us on her way over to Mouse. Our heads turn one at a time as she slowly passes by. Our eyes linger on her perfectly curved backside, as her sweet, heady scent fills our nostrils. It's fucking intoxicating. All of it. The entire show. Her eyes lock with mine for a second. She does a double-take. I'm used to it. No one expects that color of blue coming out of my worn face. My eyes are the only thing that don't seem to age. She recovers quickly, but she knows I noticed.

She finally gets over to Mouse. She presses her body lightly to him and whispers into his ear. I'm suddenly filled with an unwarranted jealousy. I want to rip her away from him. I don't hear what she's saying, but I hear Mouse reply, "Yeah, do your thing. I've got your back if you miss." He puts his hand on her waist and pulls her a little closer as he answers. My jealousy is overflowing now.

"What in the damn hell are you doing?" Butch brings me back to reality. "If you get any closer to him, you're going to render him useless as your teammate. Mousie won't be able to walk soon."

"I'm discussing strategy with my teammate. You're familiar with strategy, right?"

Damn, does that mean she knows what we do for a living? It kind of disappoints me.

"The only strategy Mouse is going to need is how to hide what's going on in his pants right now," Hawk says from the corner. We all laugh at the honesty of it. The rest of us are getting hard just watching her, much less touching her.

"Do y'all want to talk all night or play pool?" she purrs, suddenly throwing in a Southern accent. She knows who she's dealing with. A lot of us are Southerners or Texans. She's using all of her ammunition.

"Okay, Strawberry Shortcake, let's see your stuff," Butch says.

It's not until now as she moves directly under the light that

I notice her blonde hair has flicks of red running through it. Her hair, like the rest of her, is perfect. She looks like a fucking angel to me.

She puts a hundred down on the table and waits patiently for the rest of us to follow. I'm so mesmerized. I temporarily forget that I'm expected to play in the game. I fumble for my hundred and finally put it down on the table.

"Y'all okay if I break?" she asks as JJ picks up the money and starts to rack the balls. I'm back in game mode now. I nod to the table without saying anything. Ladies first.

She walks over to the head of the table and bends over slightly. Thank God I'm not standing behind her. I would be rendered useless. Bryce's eyes are laser-focused on her ass. I think he might be in shock. I look up to see her about ready to break. Her eyes lock with mine. She breaks without looking away from me. It's so fucking sexy.

"Stripes," she says. I finally look at the table. Perfect break. I think we're about to get hustled.

She moves around the table with military precision. The striped balls are falling into the pockets like obedient soldiers. It takes her about five minutes to clear the table. I'm guessing she's done it faster, but I can tell this is more of a show to her than a competition. And all of us are enjoying every last minute of it.

"Eight ball, top left." She gestures slightly toward the target pocket.

Straight in. I'm not even sure it touched the sides. She straightens up, puts her stick on the table, and walks over to JJ to collect her winnings. He's fanned the bills out like playing cards against his chest. He's going to make her work for it.

She looks at him directly in the eyes and plucks the bills out of his hands slowly, one by one. God, she has balls. There aren't many men who would stare at JJ that long.

She walks over to Mouse and gives him his two hundred and a little wink. He winks back. I'm not liking where I think this is headed. But then, just as suddenly as she approached us, she walks away.

"Thanks for the game, boys," she says, the Southern accent gone.

"What? That's it?" Butch says. "We don't get a chance to win our money back?"

"Maybe another time. I need to get some rest. I have a big meeting in the morning." She looks right at me when she says it, knowing I should have figured it out by now.

I watch her hand her two hundred to Pete. "I'm picking up their drinks tonight," she says, nodding over to us as she walks out of the bar.

And then it hits me, like a grenade blowing up in my face. Her meeting tomorrow is with me, with us. She's our new CIA agent.

Well, this is just going to be fucking inconvenient.

Chapter Ten

Mack was two months into a three-month deployment in Iraq. The last month was always the toughest on him. He had to actively manage his excitement about seeing Millie again soon, so he could stay focused on his job. Lack of focus could get him or his teammates killed, but every day he got closer to seeing Millie, he felt like he lost just a little bit of his clarity.

Millie made him drawings for every day he was gone on deployment with countdown numbers on the top of each one. Mack pulled that day's drawing out first thing every morning. They became like a lifeline to him. Beatrice helped Millie count out how many drawings she would need, and then helped her pack them into an envelope for Mack to take with him when he left. Beatrice always had a soft spot for Mack growing up. It had transferred over to Millie. At least she was able to protect Millie from absorbing too much of Camille's crazy while he was gone.

"Let me see today's drawing," Chase said. He was Mack's team leader.

Mack held up the drawing of a butterfly. At least half of Millie's artwork had something to do with butterflies.

"She's quite the little Picasso already. Maybe she can be an artist," Chase said, smiling. "Although it seems like you're already training her for the military. How's it going?

"She's a crazy good swimmer already. Decent shot for as little as her hands are," Mack said proudly. "The only thing I'm worried about is her self-defense skills. She's not taking to it."

"She's only eight years old, dumbass. She doesn't need to be a Krav Maga master just yet," Chase said, rolling his eyes.

Mack knew Chase was messing with him, but he really was getting worried about Millie's lack of interest in his self-defense training. She'd taken so readily to swimming and shooting, but he couldn't get her to focus on hand-to-hand defense.

"If you're trying to make her the first female SEAL, I think Demi Moore already beat her to that," Harry chimed in from the corner of the room.

Mack laughed. There was little to no chance of that. First, he'd never allow her to be in the military. He was training her purely to take care of herself in the civilian world, especially if something happened to him. And second—and more importantly—she had the focus of a drunk bird. As she'd gotten older, their conversations had started to physically wear Mack out. Following her train of thought was like watching a pin ball bounce unrestrained through the machine.

Last time he was home, he'd been working with her on

perfecting an army crawl. He bought a pair of fake night-vision goggles so they could try an assault in the dark. He told her to crawl through the corn stalks in Camille's garden to see if she could sneak up on him undetected. After waiting ten minutes for her to crawl only fifty feet, he decided to flank her. He snuck around from the back and started crawling through the garden to surprise her. He was twenty feet away when he heard her singing. He got closer to find her on her back—goggles on top of her head—looking up at the stars through the stalks. He grabbed her foot before she even knew he was anywhere near her. She definitely didn't have a future as a special forces operator.

"You know it's been eight years, man," Chase said quietly. "There's nobody coming for her. You need to pull back the defenses a little."

"Yeah, I know, but even just in everyday life, you know, if I'm not here, I want her to be able to protect herself," Mack said.

"Nothing's going to happen to you, but if it does, I've got her. Mariel and I will make her one of our own. You know that," Chase said.

"And if you're gone, too, what happens then?"

"Then Harry's got her or Clem, and on down the line. You know how this works. She's family. Someone's always going to have her back," Chase said.

"I don't want Clem anywhere near my daughter. Ever. No matter the circumstances."

"Roger that," Chase said, laughing as he headed to the showers.

Chase was Mack's best friend. They'd known each other

since Mack joined Chase's team. He knew Chase would die defending him but more importantly, he'd die defending Millie. Chase was the only one who knew the entire story, and he'd never told anyone, not even his wife.

Mack remembered the day he'd received the phone call telling him he had a daughter. The man on the other end of the phone spoke with a heavy Slavic accent that made it almost impossible for Mack to understand what he was saying. Mack finally recognized he was talking about Nejra, the woman he'd worked with when his team was assigned to Sarajevo. The man said Nejra had gotten pregnant with Mack's baby. He had slept with her several times, but he'd always used protection, so his first thought was that her family was trying to shake him down for money.

The man continued, telling him that Nejra's brother had murdered her in an honor killing. Nejra was Muslim, and Mack knew she had a brother. He guessed it could be a possibility, but he didn't think it seemed likely. Nejra had told him that she was very close to her brother. The man told him the brother was going to kill the baby if Mack didn't come over to Bosnia to get her. Now, Mack just thought it was a set up to kill him for sleeping with Nejra.

The man quickly hung up without leaving his name or number. Luckily, he had called Mack at the base. Mack had the intelligence team trace the call. He only had to do a little research on the man who had called to figure out his connection to Nejra was legitimate. And he found out, sadly, that Nejra had died, although the official cause of death was listed as natural causes.

Chase advised him vehemently against going over to

Bosnia, but he knew Mack was determined, even if he had to go AWOL. There was something in Mack's gut that made him think the man on the phone was telling the truth. Chase gave him two weeks' leave, telling everyone that Mack had to handle a family matter.

Mack located the baby within a day of being in Sarajevo. Nejra's brother still had her. By what Mack had been able to put together, the baby had to be at least two months old. If the story was true, he wondered why the brother hadn't killed the baby yet. Mack observed them for almost a week. The brother took the baby out with him when he left the building to go to the market or visit friends, but he always left her in the apartment when he went for prayers at the mosque.

Mack spent days trying to determine how to decide if the baby was his without tipping anyone off. He'd almost decided to confront the brother when one day, he caught a glimpse of the baby's bright red hair through his binoculars. A bolt of electricity surged through his body. He knew right then that the baby was his.

Mack waited for the next time the brother left for the mosque, and just walked in and took the baby. He realized he was committing an international crime that could land him in jail for life or get him killed, but he didn't care. His gut was telling him this was his baby, and he wanted to get her out of there.

He flew all the way back to New York without anyone questioning him. He told everyone his wife had died in child-birth, and that he was taking the baby home. The flight attendants flocked around the baby the entire flight, helping him feed and change her. Mack had little idea what to do with a baby, so they saved him.

Mack had a paternity test done first thing when they got to New York. She was a hundred percent his. He hadn't really considered what he would do if she wasn't. He had felt certain she was his daughter since the day he saw her hair, and the feeling had grown stronger the moment he picked her up off the floor of that apartment.

After he got her a birth certificate in New York, he'd spent a few days with Millie alone in Virginia Beach before going down to the Outer Banks to try to convince Camille to take care of her. He and Chase agreed it was probably the safest place for Millie in case anyone was following him.

Mack had lived on pins and needles for almost two years after he'd brought her back, but slowly over the years, his fear had almost gone away. He still jumped every time he heard a Slavic accent of any kind, but thankfully, in Virginia Beach and the Outer Banks, that didn't happen very often.

Chapter Eleven

MILLIE, VIRGINIA BEACH, VIRGINIA, 2019

As I drive up to the naval base, my palms begin to sweat. My mind is racing. My heart feels like it's going to beat right out of my chest. I've never had a panic attack, but I'm sure this is what it feels like.

"Ma'am, can I help you?" The guard's talking to me, but my mind is still spinning from thinking about the last time I pulled up to this gate. It was eight years ago, but it suddenly feels like yesterday.

"Ma'am?" The guard leans down, and looks cautiously into my open window.

"Sorry. Yes, I'm here to meet with Harrison Culver. Captain Culver," I say, trying to keep my voice from shaking.

"Name?"

"Harrison Culver."

"I mean your name, ma'am." He's looking at me like I'm an idiot. Or I'm high. Or both.

"Oh, right. Sorry. Millie Marsh." I suddenly feel sixteen years old again.

"Wait here." He walks back to the guard gate.

I force myself not to look over at the last place I saw Dad. Where he dropped me off at my car. Where he told me he'd see me in a few days. My eyes are focused firmly on my steering wheel when the guard walks back over.

"You can go in. Captain Culver is expecting you at eight hundred. Do you know where you're going?"

I try to focus as he gives me directions to Culver's office. Apparently, I didn't focus well enough. I have to text Raine to give me directions again. She's waiting for me as I get out of my car.

"I see you're wearing your super agent costume," Raine says, smiling. I'm wearing a black pantsuit, white button-up blouse, hair up in a top knot, glasses, and heels. My power look.

"Yeah, I need all the mojo I can get right now."

"You okay? I know you're feeling some kind of way being here."

"I think I'm okay. I just don't want to talk about him. I'm focused."

Raine takes me in the building, and we wind through a bunch of hallways. Every time I take a turn, I see guys with long hair, scraggly beards, scars, tats, tired eyes. This is going to be harder than I thought. We finally stop at an open door. The guy at the desk looks up. His eyes widen when he sees me.

"Captain, this is Millie Marsh," Raine says. "She's the

agent we talked about who will be running the target package for Amar Petrovic in Sarajevo."

Culver walks around his desk, smiling at me with a kinder smile than is necessary. As he's shaking my hand, he says, "Raine, may Agent Marsh and I have a moment alone?"

"I'm briefed on this package, sir," Raine says quickly.

"I know you are, Raine. I still need a few minutes." Culver's eyes are so intensely focused on me that I think they might start shooting out laser beams soon.

"I'll be right out here," Raine says as she closes the door slowly.

Culver motions me to take a seat, and retreats back behind his desk. He sits down and just stares at me. Right through me. "So, it's Agent Marsh now, huh?"

I suddenly feel a little uneasy. "I'm sorry. Have we met?"

He smiles at me knowingly. "Millie, I know you're Mack's daughter."

I take a deep breath. I wonder how he found out. Did George tell him? Did Raine? Someone's been talking too much.

"And I know your dad wouldn't want you here," he continues.

"You knew my dad?" I say slowly.

"I was at his funeral, Millie. I talked to you there. You've grown up, but you haven't changed that much." His eyes are still intense, but he's smiling at me now.

"I don't remember much about that day," I say, looking down.

Actually, I don't remember a thing about that day. I was

still in shock, and what little did register with me back then, I've worked hard to forget.

"He wouldn't want you here," he repeats. "He didn't want you in this life. Not even close to it."

"Well he isn't here anymore," I say bluntly.

"I called Chase when I found out you were coming down here. He thought you were living in London. He didn't even know you were in the CIA."

I lived with Chase and his family for months after Dad died. They quite literally saved me. I couldn't have survived it all without them.

"Yeah, we lost touch," I say, not meeting Culver's eyes.

"He said you lost touch when you left for college. You stopped returning his calls, and then your phone number didn't work at all. He was your dad's best friend. You know that. You lived with them for months after . . ." His voice fades away. He saw my face the first time he mentioned my dad dying. He's trying to avoid that again.

"I chose to move on. I had to move on. And this has nothing to do with why I'm here," I say, finally looking up.

"Are you sure? Chase seemed pretty upset that you were coming here. He wanted to know what the target package was," Culver says. "I couldn't tell him because he doesn't have clearance anymore, but he asked me if it had anything to do with Bosnia. Why would he ask me that? What's he not telling me?"

Well, at least, now I know Chase didn't tell him. I look at Culver directly in the eyes. "I have no idea why he would ask that. Maybe he's still in contact with someone here, and they tipped him off."

"You're lying to me, Millie," Culver says carefully. "Chase is lying to me, too. I don't like that. But I guess that's where we're at, and frankly, if you're up to something, I want to be the one in charge of you. I owe that to your dad."

"I'm not up to anything. I just need to get Petrovic. I would do it alone if I could. Believe me, I don't want to be back here," I say, trying to control the harsh tone in my voice.

"From what I remember Mack telling us, you might have the skills to do it alone. He said he had you trained up on everything we do here. Are you still a dead-eye shooter?"

"I don't shoot very much anymore."

I don't do anything that I used to do with my dad. I had to shut down everything that reminded me of him.

"I read through your file," Culver says. "One of the top interrogators in the agency after only three years. Impressive. And you speak several languages, including Bosnian. Why Bosnian?"

He's still trying to dig for information. He knows I'm lying. He's good at this. Way better than most people.

"I lived in a predominantly Bosnian neighborhood when I was at NYU. I just picked it up. Languages come easy to me."

"Huh," he says, looking up from my file. "Well, it's a nice coincidence then that your first target is Bosnian."

I just stare back at him. Anything I say now will confirm I'm lying.

"Millie, the information you have on Petrovic looks solid. The target package is legitimate, but please tell me if there's anything else I need to know. You know from your dad how these teams work. We need all of the information."

"My dad never talked about his time here. I don't know

anything about how you work. And everything you need to know is in my package."

"I notice that there's no mention of your parents or your family in your file. I know the agency tries to hide any relationships to high-ranking military officials or special operators for your safety if you're captured. That's why they omitted it, right?"

"Yep, that's it," I say quickly. "And I'd appreciate if we could keep it between us. Did any of the other guys work with my dad?"

"The team leader, Mason Davis, was in the pipeline by that time, but he was still in San Diego, and just a rookie. Different squad. He probably won't put it together. I think you should tell him though. The entire team really. They'd like to know that you're part of this family."

"I'm not part of this family." My eyes start to water again, so I look down. Oddly, I cry as much when I'm frustrated as when I'm sad, and I'm starting to get really frustrated. I wanted to fly under the radar here, get the job done, and get back to D.C.

"You're part of the family whether you think you are or not. It's just the way it is. But I won't tell them if you don't want them to know," Culver says, standing up. "I have another meeting right now. Be back here tomorrow morning for a briefing at eight. You can meet the team and read them into the package. Bring a go-bag. Sounds like we're going to be wheels up pretty quickly on this one."

He gets up to open the door for me, but stops at my chair first. He leans down and looks me directly in the eyes. "Millie, your dad was one of the best guys I've ever met. He saved my life more than once. You can hate me, hate the SEALs, hate all of this, but I will die myself before I let anything happen to you. Do you understand that?"

I just nod my head. I don't trust my voice.

Chapter Twelve

MASON, VIRGINIA BEACH, VIRGINIA, 2019

Culver wants to see me, so I head over to his office. As I'm rounding the corner, I see Raine standing by the door.

"You in this meeting, too?" I say as I glance in Culver's window, and see the back of the mirage's head. She has her hair up in a twisty thing, but there's no mistaking that strawberry blonde color.

"No. I'm just waiting for my colleague from the agency. She's the one who's here to brief you on the op in Sarajevo," Raine says, confirming my suspicion.

We both look over as the door opens. The mirage walks out, and looks right at me, smiling, her green eyes sparkling. I can already tell she has a mischievous streak, and it's sexy as fuck.

"Master Chief, nice to see you again," she says with not a hint of a Southern drawl. She's trying to be all business now.

"Miss Marsh."

She's wearing a suit, heels, and glasses, trying to cover up the sex appeal she ladled out like soup last night. It's not working at all.

"Agent Marsh." She corrects me, and gives me a quick once over.

Damn. The way she just unabashedly looked at my body makes me want to throw her up against a wall and take her right here.

"My bad. Agent Marsh," I say, forcing myself not to look at the opening of her blouse. "You hustle anyone else at pool last night?"

"Hustle? I think you mean play a completely honest and principled game of pool against inferior opponents," she says, smiling.

"No, that's not what I meant at all." I smile back at her as Culver joins us quickly. He looks at me like he might pull out his sidearm and put it between my eyes.

"I see you two have already met," Culver says, firing the words out like bullets.

I step back and motion Millie past me. "You owe me another game to win my money back."

"Only if I can break," she says.

She turns around and smiles at me, and turns back around in one graceful, fluid motion. I leer at her as she walks down the hall with Raine.

Culver sees how I'm looking. "If you're ready for our meeting, Master Chief," he says curtly, motioning me to take a chair.

I barely hit the chair when he continues. "Mason, Millie's dad was a SEAL—a man who I served with, a man who saved my life. He was one of the best men I've ever known. As he's no longer with us, I feel like I can step in for him and say that if you ever touch Millie sexually or, you know, just even casually, like tapping her on the shoulder, I will kill you. Then I will take your body to my workshop, cut it up into tiny pieces, and feed the pieces to the sharks in the bay."

Ah, now I see what's caused his bad mood. "Damn, Culver. It seems like your plan is pretty advanced. I mean you've definitely wanted to kill me for a while, right?"

"I haven't, actually. Just now for the first time when I saw you looking at her like that," he says, motioning toward the door. "You know, I'd prefer you not look at her either. Or talk to her."

"We're going to work on one of her packages. I'm probably going to have to look at her and talk to her." And to be honest, I'm going to want to do a lot more to her before she leaves town.

"Keep it to a minimum. I know how you work and you know, usually, I couldn't give a shit about who you sleep with, but she's so far off-limits. So far. The furthest. You understand me?"

"I'm going to work with her. I wouldn't hook up with her anyway." It seems like the right thing to say, but I know he's not going to buy it for a second.

"Like you've never slept with someone who works with us. I've seen the looks you get around here, and again, usually, I could not care less. I do not care about your sex life. I don't want to think about it at all. But not Millie. Never Millie. Tell me you understand."

"Yeah, I got it. I got it." My brain's telling me this is probably for the best, but the rest of my body is not so sure. I think I agree with the rest of my body.

Culver's staring at me like death, so I repeat, "I got it, man. Off-limits."

"And I expect you to keep the rest of the team away from her, too," Culver says.

Yeah, a hundred percent I can promise that. None of those assholes are even going to get near her. If I can't have her, no one else can.

"Roger that," I say. "So her dad died?"

"Yeah. In Iraq. She was only a kid. Sixteen."

"How many years ago was that?"

"Like eight years. She's still not over it. She started tearing up when I mentioned him just now."

"They were close?"

"Yeah. She lived down on the Outer Banks with her grandma, but Mack got down there every chance he got. He talked about her nonstop. At his funeral, man, she couldn't even stand up. I remember it like it was yesterday. It was awful," Culver says, looking down. "She ended up staying with Mack's team leader and his wife for a while after, but then everyone lost touch with her—or more specifically, she lost touch with all of us."

"It's maybe a little weird that she joined the agency after she took his death so hard," I say. "Seems like she'd want to get away from all this."

"Yeah, I have a bad feeling that she's trying to avenge his death somehow," Culver says.

"Like how? You mean just generally? Who was responsible for his death?"

75

"They think Al-Qaeda. Mack was clearing a building in Fallujah when it exploded. We had to get out of the area before we could really determine what caused it."

"Wait, Mack Marsh? I remember him. The name anyway," I say.

I might have met him once. It seems like I did, but I definitely remember the word on him was that he was one of the toughest motherfuckers out there. It's kind of hard imagining him being a dad.

"Yeah, he was getting close to retirement when you came in," Culver says. "He was going to spend more time with Millie. He was buying a house for them. Just awful timing. But, I guess there's never good timing."

"You think she knows who was responsible for his death?"

"We'll find out tomorrow what she knows. But the group she's targeting is Yusef Hadzic's network. He has ties to Al-Qaeda. The agency's been looking for him for years, and Sayid Custovic before that. I was involved in missions for Custovic. They're ghosts, man. If she could bring Hadzic in, it would be huge. I'm thinking Custovic has to be dead."

"I read in her file that she's fluent in Bosnian. All those guys are Bosnian, right? You think there's some connection?" I ask.

"A lot of agents spoke Bosnian back in the eighties and nineties. It was more of a hot spot back then. Kind of rare for someone as young as her to have a focus in that area. But, you know, Custovic and Hadzic took up shop in Afghanistan after the war ended in Bosnia. So who knows? Just keep a close eye on her in case she's up to something."

"I thought you didn't want me to look at her."

"Professionally, watch her back. Don't let anything happen to her, but again, I swear to God, Mason, keep your hands off of her."

"Roger that." Watch her, but don't look at her. Have her back, but don't touch her back. Clear as mud.

"Look, another thing—she doesn't want anyone else to know that her dad was one of us," Culver says.

"Why not? Just makes her part of our family."

"I don't think she wants any part of us. To her, all we did was take away her dad. I don't think she's a big fan of the teams, but she needs us to get this target. Probably better for all of us to get it done quickly, and get her back to D.C. Briefing at eight hundred tomorrow," Culver says, standing up and indicating our meeting is over.

As I leave Culver's office, my feet take me toward Raine's office where I know Millie will be headquartered while she's here. My brain tells me to turn around, but I don't. She's sitting at Raine's desk, alone in the office. She looks up when she senses me at the door.

"Culver told me about your dad," I say waiting for her to reply. She just stares at me blankly. "That he was a SEAL. That he died. I'm sorry."

The way she looks at me—with wide, glassy eyes—makes me wish I hadn't said anything. "Thank you," she says, looking down as her hands grip the sides of the chair.

"Are you okay?" I walk closer to her. I'm a little concerned she's going to pass out. The color has left her face.

She looks up. Her beautiful eyes are now full of tears. "You'd think after eight years, it would get easier," she says, trying to smile. "I'm so sorry. This is really unprofessional."

"I've lost a lot of people in my life. It doesn't get easier. And you're fine. Showing your emotions isn't a weakness. It's the strongest thing you can do. You've got to feel it all or you're never going to function correctly."

I sit on the desk right beside her, reaching out to put my hand on her shoulder. Wait. What did Culver tell me about touching her? I seem to be forgetting right now. She nods but looks down again, not saying anything.

"Look, Millie, I lost my mom when I was ten. That's twenty-five years ago. The pain gets less severe, but it never goes away. The best thing to do is talk about it."

She looks up. "How many people have you talked to about your mom?"

"Exactly zero. I'm not a big talker."

"So, do as I say, not as I do," she says. At least I've gotten a little smile back on her face.

"Something like that. I'll make a deal with you. If you talk to me about your dad, I'll talk to you about my mom."

She looks at me suspiciously. "I should probably get back to my hotel, and get ready for tomorrow," she says.

She closes her computer and stands up. I haven't moved, so we're eye to eye. She's just inches away from me. I want to hug her, protect her, kiss her. It takes every ounce of discipline I have not to touch her again.

"You didn't agree to my deal—the talking deal." There are many other deals I'd like to propose to her, but this is the only one that seems appropriate right now.

"We'll see. I don't like talking about him much. But thank you. It's nice of you to offer," she says.

She walks past me to the door. I follow her because my

body won't let me do anything else. It's impossible not to be near her right now. Culver did tell me to have her back, right?

"I'll walk you to your car." I purposely say it as a statement, and not a question.

"Oh, you don't have to," she says as she turns around with a confused look on her face.

"I know I don't have to, but I want to. That's why I'm offering," I say, following her out into the parking lot.

She clicks the lock on her car. I walk past her to open it. She looks up at me, those eyes wide and innocent now. Ah, man, I'm shook. I can't even say anything.

She gets in, and as I'm closing her door, she says, "Thanks. See you tomorrow."

"Yep." It's all I can manage to say as I watch her drive out of the parking lot.

Chapter Thirteen

OUTER BANKS, NORTH CAROLINA, 2005

One of the first things Mack learned in basic training was how to remain calm in the chaos of war. He had been in hundreds of full-out firefights over the years, and had always immediately felt calm when the bullets started flying. Apparently, that strategy didn't apply to Parents' Night at Millie's grade school. He had never felt more stressed out in his life.

Because of his schedule, this was the first parent/teacher night he had attended with Millie. She hadn't let go of his hand since they got out of the car. Her face beamed with pride every time she introduced him to someone. Mack, on the other hand, was overwhelmed with the scene. There were kids running wildly everywhere, parents yelling at them to stop, and teachers trying desperately to be heard above the din.

"How you doing there, Mack?" Carol said. Mack turned around to find Millie's friend's mom standing behind them—her eyebrows raised and lips pursed tightly. She knew how loud noises triggered him.

"Is it always like this?" Mack asked as he tried to smile.

"It'll calm down in a few minutes when the tours and teachers' meetings start. The kids will go down to the cafeteria for pizza," Carol said, patting his arm.

Millie instinctively hugged Mack. She could sense when he was becoming tense. It rarely happened, but sometimes when a car backfired or a balloon popped, he jumped. She didn't know why. She guessed he just didn't like loud noises. And she knew that fireworks with him on the Fourth of July were completely out of the question. It's just something she had come to accept.

Thankfully for Mack, all the kids finally started filing out to the cafeteria. Millie gave him one more squeeze, and then skipped away with Chloe. Mack spent so much time alone with Millie when he visited. It was weird for him to see her as this confident, independent socialite. It made him proud and scared all at the same time.

Mack showed up fifteen minutes early for his scheduled appointment with Millie's teacher, and ended up having to wait thirty minutes because she was running behind. *On time is late. These people would never make it in the military,* Mack thought as he stood impatiently against the lockers.

Finally, the teacher's door opened. A woman who looked like she was barely old enough to be out of school herself greeted him.

"Mr. Marsh? I'm Millie's teacher, Miss Dunning," she said, shaking his hand.

Mack followed her in and took the chair by her desk. He didn't know why he was so nervous.

"The first thing I'm going to tell you about Millie is that

she's one of my favorite students ever," she started. "And you might think that's something I say to everyone, but I don't. Millie's special, so whatever you're doing, keep doing it."

Mack felt a surge of relief go through him like someone had just told him the results of a test for a life-threatening disease had come back negative.

"Thank you." Mack couldn't think of anything more to say. He felt oddly uncomfortable discussing Millie with someone. They had been in their own little cocoon for years, and now, he was just realizing she had an entire life outside of him.

"Specifically, I can tell you her language skills are off the charts," Miss Dunning continued.

"Yeah, she's quite the talker," Mack said, laughing.

"Well, yes, she is that, too. I was going to bring that up later, but what I'm talking about right now is foreign language. We teach all the kids Spanish here, and she excels at it. She's proficient way beyond her age group."

"She must get that from her mother," Mack said.

"Did her mom speak another language? Millie never talks about her."

Mack didn't know why he had mentioned her mom. He never mentioned her to anyone, including Millie.

"Yeah, she spoke several languages," he said shortly, hoping to move on to another subject.

Miss Dunning seemed to get the hint. She told him about Millie's impressive skills in math and writing, and that Millie needed to work a bit harder on science.

"Millie's also really athletic. Have you ever thought about signing her up for organized sports?"

Mack hadn't really thought of that at all. She still seemed like a little kid to him. He knew she could swim and run faster than just about any kid he'd seen at this age, but he'd never thought about sports for her. He'd been so consumed with hiding her, he hadn't considered that maybe it was time to let her start experiencing normal group activities.

"I've never talked to her about that. I'll ask her," Mack said, a little bit embarrassed for not thinking about this sooner.

"Well, again, Millie is amazing. She's sweet, inclusive, smart, funny. Everyone loves her, so congratulations to you for raising such a lovely human," Miss Dunning said. "We are required to tell you about any concerns, so I will tell you that some of her teachers think she's not serious enough, but really I think they mean she's a chatterbox."

Mack tried not to smile, but failed. "Yeah, she's got a lot to say—all the time. Do you want me to talk to her about it?"

"No. Not at all. Unless you want to," Miss Dunning said. "Millie has a carefree spirit that I see fade in so many kids around this age as their parents get more serious about college scholarships and athletic excellence. All of that is important, but I really feel like kids need to be kids as long as they possibly can."

Mack understood why Millie liked Miss Dunning so much. He wanted Millie to keep that spirit well beyond her childhood days.

Mack left the classroom and headed down to the cafeteria to meet Millie. He opened the door to find the chaos had returned. Kids were flying around everywhere. He couldn't see Millie, but he saw Carol over in the corner of the room and joined her.

As they discussed the results of their respective parent-teacher conferences, Mack located Millie across the room talking to a few girls her age. He saw a boy trying to get her attention. She was ignoring him, but he was being pesky. Mack watched as the boy grabbed Millie's ponytail and pulled her hard toward him. Mack leaped out of his chair, ready to grab the kid and throw him across the room. Carol raced after Mack and positioned herself in front of him. She put her hand lightly on his chest.

"Mack, Mack, no, no, no. She's fine," Carol said quietly. "They're just playing, just roughhousing. Millie's strong. She can take care of herself."

Mack stopped just in time to watch Millie put an elbow in the boy's gut and return to the group of girls without missing a beat.

Hell yeah, she can take care of herself, Mack thought proudly as he allowed Carol to gently herd him back to the adult side of the room.

"Sorry," he said as he sat down next to Carol. "It's just instinct."

"I know. You're all good," Carol said. "Just remember, you're at a grade school, not in Iraq. I know it's hard to separate them sometimes."

Mack tried to smile, but she had no idea how hard it was. No one did unless they had experienced war.

"Mack, you know, if anything ever happens to you, I love Millie. I know you have other friends, but I'd be happy to take care of her. At least I'd be better than Camille," Carol said.

Mack managed a forced smile again. He hated thinking about how Millie would fair without him.

"Thanks. I really do appreciate that. And, yeah, you'd definitely be better than Camille," he said, patting Carol's hand. "I'm going to get Millie. It's about time to go home."

Mack gave Carol's hand a final squeeze as he walked over to Millie.

"Hey, Mills, are you ready? We should probably head home," he said, putting his arm around her shoulder while glaring at the ponytail puller who was still nursing his gut.

Millie grabbed Mack's hand as they walked out of the building toward the parking lot.

"Daddy, do you love Miss Carol? Are you going to marry her?" Millie asked.

"What? No, Millie, I don't love Miss Carol, and we're not going to get married," Mack said as he playfully pulled her toward him and gave her a bear hug. "Why do you say that?"

"You were holding her hand," Millie said. "I saw you."

"I wasn't holding her hand. I was touching her hand. There's a difference. She needed comforting, and that's all I was doing."

"You kiss me when I need comforting," Millie said. "You should try that with Miss Carol."

"Maybe it's time for you to stop talking now, Millie," Mack said, laughing as he squeezed her tighter.

Chapter Fourteen

MILLIE, VIRGINIA BEACH, VIRGINIA, 2019

Culver was right yesterday when he said Dad wouldn't want me here. He wouldn't want me in Virginia Beach, and he definitely wouldn't want me on the base. He always told me to stay as far away from this life as possible. He had plans that after he retired, we would move out to San Diego where he had trained. He'd buy a little house near the beach. I could go to college. We'd go surfing on my downtime. I had a calendar in my bedroom counting down the days until that happened. We only had fifty-four more days when he died.

I'm thinking of this as I lay in the hotel bed wide awake at five in the morning. My briefing with the team isn't until eight, but I can't sleep, more than partially because I'm afraid of being late. I'm perpetually ten minutes late to everything. Not five. Not fifteen. Always ten. I'm not sure how it works out that way, but it used to drive my dad crazy. He told me that in the teams, being on time was considered being late. He was always everywhere at least fifteen minutes early.

I'm so pleased with myself when I pull into the base parking lot thirty minutes early. I walk into the briefing room, and everyone is already there. They all turn to look at me like I'm late. Seriously? I never would have made it in the military.

Culver motions to me to join him in the front of the room. As I walk over, I see Mason staring at me. He smiles when I look over, and doesn't look away. His laser-focused eyes follow me the entire way across the room. The way he looks at me is intoxicating and unsettling all at the same time.

Culver walks over to greet me, and then turns to the team. "Gentlemen, this is Agent Marsh. She has what could be an extended target package starting in Bosnia, extending to Afghanistan. We've been tasked with helping her through this process. Agent Marsh, if you'd like to brief us on your first target."

"Good morning," I say. "I sincerely hope you're better operators than pool players."

Mason laughs. The rest of them narrow their eyes, looking at me like they're trying to figure out a particularly hard word in a crossword puzzle.

Mouse's face slowly breaks into a grin. "Wait. What? You're my pool partner from the other night."

"Yes, and you're welcome for the money I won you," I say.

There it is. I see the slow recognition finally make its way around the room. JJ doesn't look amused, but in fairness, I'm not sure he ever does. Raine was right about him—straight-up intimidating. The rest of them kind of laugh and roll their eyes at me.

"If whatever this is, is done," Culver says, gesturing curtly with his hands, "can we get on with it?"

"Of course, Captain. Thank you," I say. "Our first target is Amar Petrovic—a Bosnian national who's been living in Spain for the past twenty years. He recently moved his family back to Sarajevo where he grew up."

"War criminal?" Bryce asks. "I thought we got most of those a decade ago."

"He's not a war criminal. We think he has ties to the Hadzic Network," I say.

"Yusef Hadzic? Again? The CIA has been chasing him since before Brycie over there was even born," Butch says.

"And Sayid Custovic before that," Mason says, looking directly at me. There's no way he can know Custovic is my ultimate target, but he's looking at me smugly like he knows every thought I've ever had in my life.

"I've heard of Hadzic, but who's Custovic?" Bryce asks.

"Agent Marsh, why don't you give us the entire background starting with Custovic," Culver says. He's looking at me the same way Mason is. They're up to something.

I promised George I wouldn't bring up Custovic, but I'm not seeing a smooth way to get out of this. And technically, I didn't bring him up, so fine, let's do this.

"Okay, backing up a little bit," I say. "Sayid Custovic was born in Sarajevo. If he's still alive, he's fifty-two."

"If he's still alive?" JJ asks.

"It's the agency's official stance that Custovic is dead. He hasn't been seen in almost two decades."

"Is that what you believe, too?" Mason's challenging me. It's like he has a bug inside my head. I don't like it at all.

"I work for the agency, so, yes, I uphold their official stance," I say. The look on his face tells me he doesn't believe me.

I continue. "Backing up again, both of Custovic's parents were Bosnian Muslims killed by the Serbs right at the beginning of the war in 1992. Sayid survived, and from what we can tell, he stayed in Sarajevo until the end of the war. After that, he disappeared and eventually showed up in Pakistan where one of his cousins had relocated after the war. That's where Custovic became radicalized."

"So, he radicalized because of what happened to his parents?" Hawk asks.

"I'm not sure we know the why," I say. "We do know he formed a terrorist network with his childhood friend, Yusef Hadzic. They were essentially guns for hire at first to hunt down Serbian war criminals. They even worked with us for a brief moment. Then they were deemed responsible for a failed hit on some Army Rangers in 2000. That's when the agency broke ties, and Custovic and Hadzic ended up disappearing in the Hindu Kush. They've been hiding up there for decades. Hadzic is the accepted head of the network now, so much so that it's basically referred to as the Hadzic Network. Still smaller, high-profile hits, but they're more visibly tied to the bigger organizations now—first Al-Qaeda, and now the Taliban."

"Who funds them?" Mason asks.

"At first, they were bankrolled by Hadzic's father, Haroun. He was a very successful doctor before the war. He was last seen in Peshawar around 2000. He would be up in his eighties if he's still living. His family—daughters, grandkids—all still live in Sarajevo. His wife died about ten years ago in Bosnia of natural causes."

"So, how does Amar Petrovic figure into this?" Mason asks.

"Petrovic is a childhood friend of Custovic and Hadzic. He disappeared around the same time they did. The agency always thought he was in the mountains with them. It turns out he was living in Spain. He just moved his family back to Sarajevo earlier this year. That's where we picked up his trail again."

"So, you think Petrovic has been working with them from Spain?" JJ asks.

"We did think so, but we've tracked his last two decades in Spain, and seemingly, he led a pretty normal life. He's a dentist. Has a wife, three kids. Nothing suspicious."

"So why are we targeting him?" Hawk asks.

I start flipping through a few surveillance photos I have on the front screen. "This is Petrovic. We've been tracking him since he arrived back in Sarajevo. Every couple weeks, someone—never the same person—delivers a burner cell to him. It's always a discreet drop. After the hand off, the phone rings almost immediately. He talks for a few minutes then throws the cell away. We've picked up most of the phones he's discarded. All the calls are from different numbers, but the numbers all ping from around the Hindu Kush region around the Pakistan-Afghanistan border."

"Yeah, so that's all real suspicious, but how do you know he's talking to Hadzic?" Mouse asks.

"We don't. The agency has green-lighted this because of

his past association with Custovic and Hadzic. We just want to pick him up to question him."

"How long has Petrovic been back in Sarajevo? Why do you want to pick him up now?" JJ asks.

"As I said, our agents have been tailing him. We think one of them spooked Petrovic a couple of days ago. We have Petrovic under surveillance. He hasn't moved yet, but just in case he's getting suspicious, I want to go sooner than later."

"Well, let's go get him then," Mason says.

"Just like that?" I seriously thought I'd be here most of the day briefing and convincing them.

"That's why you're here, right? Let's get it done," Mason says.

"Wheels up in an hour, gentlemen," Culver says as the room springs to life. "Agent Marsh will brief you further on the plane."

Raine sees the confusion on my face. "That's how it happens here. They're not much for talking a problem to death. When they have good intel, they're ready to go."

"I see that. I'm used to a little more bureaucracy and red tape," I say.

"Not much of that here. Well, in this room anyway. When it's up to the team, they're all about action," Raine says. "Hey. Are you sure you're going to be okay without me?"

"I'll be fine. Just point me in the right direction."

"The right direction to where? The transport plane? God, you're seriously going to get lost just trying to find the plane that's taking you to Bosnia."

"Raine, I've never been here. How would I know where the planes are?"

"Maybe, just maybe, you might have noticed them when you drove up to the building. They're pretty big."

"Will you please turn down the snark and just show me where it is?" I say, laughing.

She grabs me by the arm, and starts pulling me toward the door when Mason looks over. He sees that we're laughing, but his face is deadly serious.

Raine straightens up quickly. "Hey, Mason. I was just going to show her where the plane is."

"I'm walking over there now. I'll show her. You ready?" He looks at me and then back at Raine, like he's about to give us after-school detention.

"Yes. Ready," I say as seriously as I can. It seems Work-Mason and Play-Mason are two entirely different people. "I'll see you later, Raine. Thanks for the help."

Raine walks away oddly quickly. I'm getting the feeling people don't like to be in Work-Mason's presence any longer than necessary. Mason motions me to follow him. At least, I think that's what he's doing. I look around for help and see Hawk.

"Am I supposed to follow him?" I ask.

"I probably wouldn't. The last person who did is dead," Hawk says, passing me.

Someone grabs me by the arm and starts pushing me forward. I turn around to see Bryce. "I was the new guy a few months ago. You'll get the hang of it," he says.

Bryce doesn't stop pushing me until he's shown me where to sit on the plane, and told me to strap in. I'm getting the feeling these guys are a controlling bunch. It's weird because my dad wasn't like that at all, at least not to me. Maybe he was different at work.

After the plane takes off, everyone starts putting on their headphones and closing their eyes. I'm not tired at all, so I unbuckle and go over to what looks like the command center. I set up my computer and do some work until my eyes start blurring from the dim lights. I take a seat away from the others, shut my eyes, and try to sleep a little, but to no avail. When I open my eyes, I see Mason standing over me, handing me a cup of tea.

Chapter Fifteen

I've never been able to sleep too well on planes, especially when we're on our way to a mission. My adrenaline's always pumping full force with anticipation, but today, it's on overload with Millie on the plane.

I look over to where she was sitting when we took off. She's not there anymore. My heart jumps a little bit, thinking she's gone. Like she jumped out of the plane or something. Man, she's just messing with my mind. I survey the plane quickly and see her sitting alone on a bench, looking like she's trying, and failing, to sleep. Against my better judgment, I grab her a cup of tea and head over.

"Can't sleep?" I ask.

She looks up, her eyes dripping with fatigue. I want to lie down with her and stroke her hair until she falls asleep in my arms. Instead, I hand her the cup of tea.

"I've never been very good at sleeping sitting up. I'm a

little too keyed up anyway," she says, taking the tea. "Thank you."

"Clark has sleeping pills if you need them." I sit down beside her, careful not to touch her. Culver came along on this trip, which is unusual. He's probably looking at me through his scope right now.

"Do they help? The pills," she says.

"Not really. I never sleep very well before a mission."

I tilt my head back and close my eyes. Maybe if I'm not looking at her, it will be easier to keep my hands off her.

"So, I think I probably met your dad back in the day, but I'm not sure. I was a rookie when he was retiring, and stationed in San Diego, but I got to Virginia Beach for training a few times. I definitely remember the name, but I'm not sure if we crossed paths."

"Is this your attempt to get me to talk about him?" I hear a little bit of sass coming out in her voice, and it's making me want to look at her eyes because I know they're sparkling again.

"Yes. Is it working?" I keep my eyes firmly shut.

"I think the deal was that you tell me one thing about your mom, and then I'll tell you one thing about my dad."

"I'm not sure we agreed on that order, but okay. Uhh, let's see," I say. "My mom had two kids, and she named us Mason and Dixon."

"Wait, like the Mason-Dixon line? That's amazing."

She laughs. I have to look at her. I open my eyes, and she's looking right at me. Yep, the eyes are like firecrackers again.

"Yeah. She was born and raised in Alabama, and just

Southern down to her core. I'm not sure she paid any attention to anything that went on above the Mason-Dixon line."

"She definitely would have gotten along with my grandma then," she says, laughing.

"Your turn. Tell me something about your dad."

"Wait, I thought you grew up in Texas," she says.

"I did. My parents met in college and moved back to Houston, where Dad grew up. I'm all Texas, but Mom was all Alabama. And, quit trying to get out of our deal. Tell me something about your dad."

The firecrackers die out. She takes a deep breath.

"Okay, umm," she says slowly. "He used to sing 'Layla' to me as a lullaby."

"Like Clapton's 'Layla'?"

"Yeah. Well, into my teens. If something was upsetting me or I just couldn't fall asleep, he'd start singing that, and I'd drop off like I had been hypnotized. It always worked."

"He had good taste. I love that song. One of my favorites."

"Yeah, it used to be one of mine. I still have dreams about him singing it, and he's always singing that same verse, you know 'Make the best of the situation before I finally go insane . . .'"

"'Please don't say we'll never find a way, and tell me all my love's in vain.'" I finish the verse for her.

"Yeah. I always wake up sweating and startled. It's not a good dream. It's more like a nightmare," she says in a whisper.

I reach out and take her hand in mine. I don't even care if Culver's looking. I want her eyes to look happy again.

She smiles at me, and lets me hold her hand. "I thought you said this got easier."

"I know it doesn't seem like it, but it does, eventually," I say. "Does your mom live in North Carolina?"

"I never knew my mom. She died right after I was born. I lived with my grandma growing up, and my dad got down to see me as much as he could. The worst times were when he was on deployment. But you know about that. Are you married? Kids?"

"I was married, but we never had kids."

"How long have you been divorced?"

"A while. I haven't talked to her in years. You know when you don't have kids, there's not much of a need to talk. Are you married?"

"No. Never been. I've been dating someone for a few years, but I'm not really interested in marrying him," she says.

"Does he know what you do for a living?"

"He thinks I work for the State Department."

I laugh. "I guess it's kind of hard to have any kind of relationship when one of the first things you tell him is a lie. I've been there."

"Yeah. They always say not to date someone you work with, but maybe it's easier. At least everyone knows the truth."

"Are you hitting on me?" I ask, sincerely hoping the answer is yes. Let's just get on with this thing.

"I meant someone else at the agency," she says, laughing.

"Nah, man. You can't date a spook."

"I am a spook."

"Yeah, but you're the weirdest spook I've ever met."

"What does that mean?"

"Not weird," I say slowly. "I mean, most unusual. Like most of the agents we get are skinny, and pale, and tired looking. Like zombies. You're more robust."

"Robust? What the fuck? No wonder you're divorced." She takes her hand away from mine and slugs me in the shoulder with it. She's got a decent jab.

"No, it's a compliment! Like you look healthy," I say, trying to explain myself by gesturing at her body. By the way she's looking at me, I'm guessing that wasn't the best idea.

"Damn, I hope you shoot better than you communicate," she says, shaking her head.

"Wow, that's how we're playing. Okay," I say, laughing as I rest my head back on the seat.

We sit there in silence for a second, our eyes closed.

"Can I ask you a question?" she asks slowly.

"Anything."

"My dad told me once that when he drove down to see me, he'd give himself until the Virginia-North Carolina state line to turn his work side off, so when he got home, he was just my dad. Is that even possible for you guys?"

I want so badly to tell her yes, but I don't want to lie to her. "No, it's probably not. I mean I'm sure he tried his hardest, but it's not possible to turn it off all-together. It's just not."

I look over at her. She's nodding with her eyes still closed, but I can tell she's sad again. I reach over and put my hand on top of hers.

"Try to get some sleep, Millie," I say quietly.

Chapter Sixteen

MILLIE, SARAJEVO, BOSNIA, 2019

When we arrived at the U.S. Embassy in Sarajevo, Mason and the team left immediately to pick up Petrovic. Officially, the Bosnian government didn't give us permission to take him against his will, but they had given permission for us to detain him for a "voluntary" interview. I asked to go along with them, so I could just interview him in his apartment. Culver flatly denied my request.

I'm waiting in the embassy garage for the team to return with Petrovic. I watched them pick him up from his apartment on their body cam footage. He hadn't resisted at all, which I thought was beyond odd.

The truck pulls back into the garage. Hawk, Bryce, Ty and Mason spill out. Bryce reaches back in to pull Petrovic out. He hands him off to the embassy staff who are waiting to take him to the interview room.

"He was exactly where you said he'd be. No resistance at

all," Mason says like he's just come back from a walk in the park.

"I know. I watched the feed. Impressive work. You guys are very efficient."

"It's just what we do every day," he says.

"It might be every day to you, but it's impressive, no matter how humble you want to be."

He shrugs, sincerely not needing the compliment. He knows they're the best in the world.

"I guess it's time for me to do my work now," I say, heading toward the interrogation room. Mason follows me.

A guard stands blocking the door, arms crossed in front of him.

"I don't want you in the room with me," I say to the guard.

"It's standard operating procedure, ma'am," the guard says.

"Well, my standard operating procedure is to be alone in the room with my subjects, so that's how we're going to do it."

The guard looks at Mason for help.

"Stand down," Mason says. "We can react from here if necessary."

The guard immediately takes a step sideways to clear the door.

"We?" I ask.

"Yeah, I thought I'd stay and watch you work. You mind?" Mason says, trying to be subtle. He clearly doesn't trust me alone in the room with Petrovic. I guess he doesn't know I've done this hundreds of times.

"Knock yourself out," I say, walking into the room.

I immediately turn off the intercom system, so Mason can't hear our conversation. I'm trying to honor George's wish as much as I possibly can.

Petrovic looks up at me when I walk in the room. He's clean-cut and impeccably dressed. Not at all like my usual interviewees.

"Where's Sayid Custovic?" I say in Bosnian.

Predictably, my question is met with silence, but he has already given me the answer. When you do enough interrogations, you notice everything about your subject—an eye twitch, neck muscles tensing, a head movement. With Petrovic, it was just a subtle widening of his eyes when he heard Custovic's name. Many people wouldn't have noticed, but to me it just screamed, "She knows he's alive."

"Amar," I say slowly. "I appreciate you volunteering to come in to talk to me today. It's a great first step, but I really need for you to be forthcoming with me. Where's Sayid Custovic?"

He hesitates for a second, but then says in English, "I don't know who that is."

I continue in Bosnian. "You lived next door to him when you were young. Do you forget your childhood friends that easily?"

Eye twitch. "My English is not good," he says in Bosnian. "I meant to say I haven't seen him since childhood. I heard that he's dead."

"No, Amar. He's not dead."

"I have not seen him," he says, looking down.

"That might be true, but I know you've talked to him. I've

been following you for months now. All those burner phones you drop in the trash. I have those now."

He pushes his chair back from the table like he's trying to distance himself from that information. He's really not good at this.

"I know you saw one of my colleagues grab your phone from the trash last week. He covered it pretty well, so you let it go. You should have gone with your instincts. You could be in Afghanistan with Sayid by now."

He looks down again, staring at his feet.

"Here it is, Amar. Your wife and kids are at home right now. Your neighbors saw you leave with us. Do you think that's going to get back to Sayid? I'm going to say it will. And then what happens to your family? You're his best childhood friend, so Sayid might not kill them, but he's changed a lot since you knew him. So, I'd say there's about a 60/40 chance that they're dead before we're even done talking. I have people standing by that can get them and bring them here."

"I don't know where he is." He sighs as he looks up. I sincerely feel sorry for him, which doesn't happen much. There's something about him that I can't quite put my finger on.

"But, you have talked to him."

"Yes," he whispers.

"And, you don't know where he is?"

"I swear I don't. He doesn't say, and I don't ask. I don't want to know. I haven't see him in twenty years."

"But, he still calls you. Why?"

"I don't know. A few months ago, right after I moved back to Sarajevo, a man handed me a phone, and told me to answer it when it rang. I did, and it was Sayid. Until that moment, I really did not know if he was dead or alive. We talked about nothing that day—about childhood and things we had done when we were boys. When he was done talking, he told me to throw away the phone, and he would be in touch again. Someone has handed me a phone about every month since then. The people come out of nowhere. There's no pattern. They just appear."

"And, he's never discussed where he is or what he's doing now?"

"Never, not once. I don't ask. He just reminisces. About childhood. Telling the same stories over and over again. I just listen. Like a therapist. I don't want to talk to him. I know what he's become. But, what choice do I have?"

I'm done. I have the information I wanted from him—that Custovic is still alive. I believe he's telling the truth about not knowing where he is.

"I'll have our people pick up your family. They should be here in a few hours. You'll need to decide if you want to stay in Sarajevo or go somewhere else. I know it might be dangerous for you if Custovic finds out you talked to us. We can take you back to Spain or somewhere else if you want that."

As I start to stand up, he reaches across the table and grabs my arm. As Mason charges into the room, I barely hear Petrovic say, "You know he looked for you for months. We all did."

Mason grabs him and throws him against the wall, pinning him there with his hand to his throat.

"Mason!" I'm trying to process what Petrovic just said,

while keeping Mason from killing him. "Mason, that's not necessary. I'm fine."

"He doesn't touch you, and that's not your call," he says as he eases up on Petrovic's throat slightly. Petrovic gasps for breath when his throat is free.

"I'm done here anyway," I say, trying to stay calm as I walk out. The guard looks at me like I should have known better. I glare at him and keep walking.

"Handcuff him to the table right now," I hear Mason say to the guard as I walk away.

"Millie," Mason says, following me.

I turn around to face him. "What the hell was that?"

"He reached for you. I reacted. I thought he was going to hurt you."

"He reached over to touch my hand to thank me for bringing his family here to him."

"I didn't know that. You turned off the sound. Why did you do that?"

"I don't have to explain my interrogation tactics to you. And, don't ever interrupt me like that again."

I'm pissed. I want to know what Petrovic said, and what he meant. But that opportunity vanished when Mason almost killed him.

"I'm sorry," he says as he grabs for my shoulder to stop me from walking away.

I shrug his hand off. "Look, Mason. This isn't personal. I let you do your job. Let me do mine."

I go back to my room, but I can't sleep. I'm thinking about what Petrovic said. *"You know he looked for you for months.*

We all did." What does that mean? Who looked for me? Who does he think I am?

It's around eleven. I decide to take another shot at Petrovic to see if I can catch him off guard. Interviewees are usually a lot more pliable when they're tired.

The guard isn't at all happy to see me at this late hour. "Ma'am, the prisoner is sleeping. Everyone is sleeping."

"First, he's not a prisoner," I say. "And, second, it's not your call. Wake him up."

He begrudgingly walks away to get him, and returns with a very groggy-looking Petrovic. I follow them into the interrogation room and tell the guard to leave the room. The guard looks at me warily. "You can cuff him to the table if it will make you feel better," I say.

He seems to be fine with that compromise. "I'll be right outside," he says, shutting the door.

"So you did hear what I said before that man attacked me," Petrovic says. "I think we should speak in Bosnian in case the guard is listening."

"I'm sure there's nothing you're going to say that he can't hear. Yes, I heard you, and I want to know what you meant."

"You look just like her," Petrovic says, letting out a long sigh like he's reminiscing on days gone by.

"Just like who?"

"Your mother."

"My mother? So, you've spent some time in New York? You knew my mom," I say flippantly.

"I know you at least suspect who she really is, who she was," he says. "It's why you're here."

Chapter Seventeen

MASON, SARAJEVO, BOSNIA, 2019

I'm having a beer with the team on the roof of the embassy when I see that guard from the Petrovic interrogation come through the door, looking around for someone. He sees me and walks over.

"Master Chief Davis," he says.

"Yeah, what are you doing up here?" This is an operator-only area. No other personnel allowed.

"I thought you would want to know that the agent from earlier tonight—the blonde woman—is with the suspect again."

"Wait, what? Agent Marsh?"

The guard nods. "She's with him right now."

"What do you mean she's with him?"

"She came down about eleven, and told me to wake the prisoner up. She wanted to talk to him again."

I glance at my phone. It's almost midnight. Why the hell did he wait so long to tell me?

"Is she alone with him?" I already know the answer, but I'm hoping someone had the sense not to let her do that again.

"Yeah. She wouldn't let us come in with her," the guard says.

I jump up. "Holy crap, I'm going to kill her."

Butch stands up with me. He's seen this look in my eyes before, and it never leads to anything good. "Everything okay, Mase? You need me to come with you?"

"The only thing I'm going to need is an alibi after I kill Agent Marsh."

Butch grabs at my arm, but I'm already through the door and down a flight of stairs. I break into a run toward the interview room. Just as I round the corner, she comes out of the room.

"What in the fuck—" I say as I'm closing in on her.

"What in the fuck am I doing?" She cuts me off. She's pissed again. "My job, Mason. I'm doing my job."

"I told you not to be alone in the room with him. I asked you to get me before you talked to him again."

"I don't work for you." She tries to walk past me, but I block her with my arm.

"While you're here—attached to my team—I'm responsible for your safety." I'm pissed, too. I don't like when people defy my orders. Usually, no one ever does.

"I relieve you of that responsibility." She tries to go under my arm. I wrap my arm around her, and hold her still. She attempts to break my grip with an quick and hard jab to my ribs. It doesn't budge me, but I'm impressed.

"You can't relieve me of the responsibility. That's not how

it works, Millie. Going into that room alone with him was dangerous."

"It wasn't, and it was the only way he was going to talk to me after you attacked him," she says. "Look, I know this is the first time we've worked together, but I've interviewed hundreds of these guys without a problem. This is my job. I know what I'm doing."

"There's always a first time. He tried to attack you this afternoon."

"He tried to touch me, Mason. He tried to touch my hand, and you tried to kill him." She tries to shrug off my arm, and I let her this time. Her eyes are telling me I've gone too far.

"Did he tell you anything else?" I try to calm my voice down to a normal level.

"Yes, he told me that Yusef Hadzic is alive. He knows where his father lives. He knows Yusef visits his father. Fucking Yusef Hadzic. We can watch the father's place, and potentially locate Yusef. No one has gotten this close in years."

"Is that who he was talking to on the burner phones? How do we know he's telling the truth?" I ask.

"We don't, but it gives us something else to go on. If I can locate the father, we can at least watch his place and hope that Yusef visits."

"Okay, well, where is he, the father?"

"Petrovic said he's in Afghanistan, in the mountains near where the network operates. He gave me a general area. I just need to try to find his house on the satellite."

"Millie, look, I'm sorry I doubted you. I feel responsible

for you while we're working together," I say, trying to bring the charged mood back down a little bit.

"You're not responsible for me, but I appreciate you having my back." Her body language and tone have softened.

"Hey. The guys are having a beer up on the roof. Do you want to join us?"

"I should really start working on this," she says starting to walk away.

I grab her shoulder. "Millie, it's past midnight. We're going to be on a ten-hour flight later today. You'll have all that time to work. Just come up and join us for one drink. I feel like I owe you a peace offering."

"Actually, I could use a drink right now."

I stand back and motion her to go before me up the stairs to the roof. I try not to focus on her ass, but not very successfully.

We reach the roof. The guys see her walking over. Butch looks relieved that she's still breathing.

"Miss Millie, I'm glad you could join us tonight," he drawls. "Can I serve you a beer?"

She takes one from him, and sits between him and Hawk.

"So, Millie, tell us a little about yourself," Butch says. "Are you married? Dating anyone?"

"Why? Are you asking me out?"

"Hell no," Butch says. "You're young enough to be my daughter or maybe a little sister."

"Yeah, she's being an annoying-ass little sister right now," I say, laughing.

She gives me a fake glare, smiling a bit. "God, if I would

have had y'all as my brothers, I never would have had one date."

"Oh yeah, you would have," Hawk says. "You just would have had one or two of us on the date with you. In fact, I think that might be a good idea right now. When's your next date? Butch here has some free time. He could be your escort. Ain't that right, Butch?"

"Well, I would just be delighted to escort you on your next date, Miss Millie," Butch says. "And, as a gesture of goodwill towards the young gentleman, I'll leave my rifle at home, and only carry my sidearm."

"Let us know where you take them for their date, Butch. We're happy to do overwatch," Bryce adds. "And I'm definitely bringing a rifle. Maybe two or three, depending on my mood."

"You know, y'all, I think I'm going to pass. And, I might just stop dating all-together," she says, smiling again.

"See what can be accomplished with teamwork? She's going to stop dating, Butch," Hawk says.

"Man, Hawk, it is my pleasure to be of service," Butch says.

She rolls her eyes at them while she accepts another beer from Butch. I watch her laugh at Hawk as he tells her a story about how he has his gun room right off the entrance to his house, so all his daughter's dates can get a good look at it before they leave with her. Like looking at Hawk isn't intimidating enough. Her eyes change quickly as he talks about his daughter. I know she's thinking about her dad again, but she's still smiling and laughing. Maybe, it's finally getting a little bit easier for her.

DONNA SCHWARTZE

Chapter Eighteen

"Dad, c'mon, I don't want to practice anymore," Millie whined as she collapsed down on the cool grass in Camille's backyard.

Mack was becoming increasingly frustrated with Millie's lack of discipline. She had been such a willing student when she was younger. She was already a better shot than most guys he knew, and she was decent at self-defense for her size. He just wanted her to be great at it.

"Millie, you have to keep up with these skills. You never know when you're going to need them," Mack said reaching under her arms to pull her up.

"I live in the Outer Banks. No one is going to attack me here. You act like I'm going on a mission with you," she said rolling her eyes.

Mack absolutely hated this new pre-teen, sassy side of Millie. Chase, who had two daughters of his own, told him to expect it, and it had arrived like a freight train barreling down the tracks.

"Millie, I've told you there is danger everywhere. You have to be prepared," Mack said, trying to control the frustration in his voice.

Mack noticed the way men had started looking at her. She was only twelve, and high school-aged boys turned their heads when she walked by. When he was around, they stopped looking real fast, but he worried about when he wasn't there with her.

"Let's try the attack from behind again. You're too slow," Mack said.

"Fine. Can we go surfing after this? Maybe do something I would actually enjoy," she said, flipping her ponytail dramatically.

"Just start walking," Mack growled as he disappeared behind the hedgerow.

Millie started walking, knowing he would jump out from behind at some point and try to pull her in. They had already done this drill five times, and she thought she nailed it every time. She walked the full length of the bushes, and he still hadn't attacked her. She sighed and turned around to find him inches from her face.

Before she could react with an uppercut to his nose, he had her arms pinned to her side and his hand over her mouth. She tried to pound her foot into his instep, but he had lifted her off the ground, so her body was dangling helplessly in the air. She flailed wildly, trying to break his hold without any success. Mack flipped her body up in the air, and then pinned her to the ground. When he saw her wide eyes starting to fill with tears, he let go of her quickly, and sat down next to her.

"Mills, I didn't mean to scare you, but that's why you can't get arrogant about this training," he said gently. "You're really strong for your size, but most guys are always going to be a little stronger. You have to be ready for them."

Despite trying desperately to stop the tears, Millie started sobbing. Mack sat her up and hugged her to his chest tightly.

"It's okay, sweetie. We can stop for today," he whispered. "Don't worry about it. I'm always going to be here to protect you. Okay?

She tried to take a deep breath between her sobs. "I k-know you're just doing this to help me. I'll try harder next time. I promise."

"What's the most important thing to remember if someone attacks you?"

"Strike hard once, put them down, and then run to get help," she said, repeating the mantra she had heard from him so many times.

"That's perfect, Millie." Mack hugged her and rubbed her back for a few minutes until her breathing returned to normal. She laid back down in the grass.

"Will you tell me something about Mom? The only thing I know is that her name was Marie," Millie said.

Mack tensed up as he always did when she brought her mom up. "C'mon, Mills. You know it makes me sad to talk about her."

Mack felt badly for lying to Millie. It didn't exactly make him sad. He just felt the less Millie knew about her mom, the safer she was going to be. She'd surprised him by asking what her mom's name was when she was only two. He'd said the first name that he thought of, Marie, which had been the name of the bank teller he had talked to a few hours earlier.

"Just tell me one thing. Like what did she look like?" Millie pleaded.

Mack sighed as he laid down by Millie in the grass. He closed his eyes to try to remember Nejra's face, but he didn't really need to think that hard. Millie looked more like her every day.

"Her eyes were green, like yours, but a little darker. And her hair was long, like to her shoulders, and brown. She was about the height you are now. Not much taller. She was little," Mack said, hoping that would be enough.

"Do I look like her?" Millie asked.

"You do look like her, and you definitely act like her. She was sweet, smart, funny, and she spoke a bunch of languages. That's probably why you're so good at Spanish."

"Did she speak Spanish?"

"No, some other languages," Mack said, wishing he hadn't brought that up.

"What languages?"

Mack knew he couldn't answer that. It would get her too close to the truth. He wished Millie was still three, so he could distract her with strawberry ice cream.

"Mills, I don't want to talk about her anymore, okay?" Mack said. "Why don't we go surfing now? I just waxed your board. It should be faster than last time."

Millie grabbed Mack's hand, and squeezed it tight. "Okay, Daddy. I'm sorry if I made you sad."

"Millie, sweetie," Mack said, squeezing her hand back. "You make me nothing, but happy, every minute of every day."

Chapter Nineteen

Since we got back to Virginia Beach, I've done nothing but stare at my computer, trying to find Haroun Hadzic's house in the area Petrovic described to me. It's the only place where I can find my next clue to Yusef Hadzic and Sayid Custovic.

Today, like the last three days, I'm not having any luck. I'm frustrated, tired, and crabby. I slam my laptop shut. What I really need is a good workout to adjust my mood. Yeah, I definitely need to sweat. Culver said I could use the base gym, so I've been bringing my workout bag every day, but I've yet to use it. It's time.

There aren't a lot of people in the gym, which is great. I like to workout alone. There are a few guys over by the weights, so I head over to the boxing bags instead. I'm maybe two minutes into my workout when a guy starts circling me like a shark looking for his next snack.

"Want me to hold the bag for you?" he asks, not even

bothering to try to hide the very slow once-over he's giving me.

"I'm good, thanks." I punch the bag extra hard for emphasis.

"Naw, you're moving the bag pretty good. You'll get a better workout if I stabilize it for you."

Not waiting for my permission, he grabs the bag, snaking his head around it to make sure his eyes are free to continue ogling. I roll my eyes at him but keep working the bag. Honestly, it is a better workout when the bag isn't swaying. I adjust my earbuds and turn the music up to drown out the little coaching tips he's offering. I'm in my zone on the bag, completely ignoring the guy, when I feel someone grab my shoulder and pull me backward. I look up to see Culver.

"Oh, hey," I say, taking out my earbud. Out of the corner of my eye, I notice the guy who was holding the bag is running away.

"What are you doing?" Culver looks at me like I've broken about twelve rules of some kind.

"What? You said I could work out in here, right?"

"Not dressed like that."

I look down to make sure I didn't forget to wear something. Nope. Yoga pants, tank top. Check. Check.

"Dressed like what?"

"Millie, this is a military base. Women are outnumbered twenty to one here. You have to watch your back. You can't encourage them."

"Oh, that's bullshit. I can't show a little bit of boob because men can't control their fucking hormones? I should be able to walk into this gym naked and not get touched."

"I swear to God, Millie. If you show up naked on this base, I will kill you myself—and I know I would have your dad's full permission to do so," he says as he motions me to walk ahead of him. "C'mon, we're going to go work out in the operators' gym."

"I thought I couldn't use the operators' gym."

"Yeah, well, we're going to make an exception. You'll be safer there."

"What? The operators aren't men?"

"The operators are men who have seen your teammates kill other men," he says. "One look from Mason or JJ, and they aren't ever going to look at you again."

As we walk into the operators' gym, Mason sees the look on Culver's face. "What's wrong? What's happening?" he says as he walks quickly over to us.

"She was getting too much attention in the base gym. Let her work out here. Kill anyone who looks at her. That includes you."

"Roger that," Mason says.

I roll my eyes at Culver. "Y'all are ridiculous."

He ignores me, and walks out.

When I turn around, Mason's looking at me. He points to my tank top. "Maybe you should wear a shirt with sleeves, and a higher neck. And thicker material."

"You're describing a turtleneck, Mason. You want me to wear a turtleneck to work out."

"Yeah, that's a great idea. And, maybe some really baggy sweatpants."

"Men are pigs."

"Yes, yes we are, and the sooner you realize that the better off you're going to be."

"Can I work out in this gym or should I hang it up for the day?" I sigh a little too dramatically. This is just adding fuel to an already frustrating day.

"You can work out here. What do you want to do?"

I look around for a bag. There isn't one. Just mainly weights. Big weights. Like The Rock-sized weights.

"I was working out with the bag in the other gym. Maybe I'll just go for a run."

"I'll work you out. I can be your bag," he says.

"You can be my bag?"

"Yeah. Kick me, punch me, do whatever. I know from the other night that you have a little self-defense training."

"Yeah, a little." Okay, I'm being humble. I have a lot of self-defense training. From what my dad taught me and the agency perfected, I'm fairly lethal for my size. But it's been a while since I used any of it, so better safe than sorry.

"Okay, let's spar," he says, like that's the most normal suggestion in the world.

"Seriously? You outweigh me by like fifty pounds." Not to mention he's a highly trained, elite fighting machine.

"Probably more than fifty, but I'll take it easy on you. Let's go." He moves over to an open area and spreads his arms wide like he's challenging me to a wrestling match. Well, this isn't going to go well for me at all, but what the hell.

I throw a few kicks and punches his way, which he blocks easily. He reaches for my arm in slow motion, trying to give me time to react. It's super condescending. I hit his arm away and jump back into a defensive mode. He smiles and lunges at me faster, grabbing at my shoulders. I throw a punch to his face, which he blocks as he spins me around into a bear hug. I elbow him sharply in the gut and stomp down on his foot with my heel.

"Ugh," he grunts, and instinctively loosens his grip. It gives me a chance to escape. I'm thinking about what Dad always told me to do at this point, but running away doesn't make sense right now.

Mason comes at me swiftly. I manage to dodge him once, and to land a hard kick in his stomach, but he barely reacts. In a second, he has me from behind, one arm around my neck in a choke-hold, the other around my waist pinning me to him. His left leg wraps around both my legs, completely immobilizing me. He kicks his left leg up a bit, lifting my feet off the ground. I'm hanging there like a helpless sack of flour. I struggle in vain a couple times, trying to loosen his grip. It doesn't work.

"Oh, okay. I give. I give," I say, frustrated.

He gently places me back on my feet and lets me go. "You move really well," he says. "Your best bet is to get away from your attacker as soon as possible though."

I take a sharp breath when I hear my dad's words coming out of his mouth. My head starts spinning.

"I think I'm done for the day," I say abruptly as I head for the door.

"Wait, Mills." He comes after me and grabs my arm. "Did I hurt you?"

And now, he's using my dad's nickname for me. It's all too much. It's too familiar.

"No, no, not at all. I'm good. I'm just worn out," I say, looking down.

"Okay," he says hesitantly as he slowly releases my arm.

I practically run out of the gym and back to my office. My head's quickly filling up with thoughts of my dad, and all of my usual blocking techniques are failing. I just need to get away from the base. I grab my computer and head out.

When I get to the parking lot, Mason's leaning against my car. Damn, this guy never stops. I mean, I guess it's part of his job description, but it doesn't translate well to personal life or to my personal life anyway. It's starting to piss me off.

"Mason, I'm fine," I say as I click the car doors open. He slides in front of my door.

"It had something to do with your dad. Tell me what it is or I'm not letting you leave."

"Mason, get out of the way. Seriously, stop." I try to open the door, but his body's blocking it.

"Nope. I'm not moving until you tell me."

"This is really obnoxious. I mean, seriously, you're being a bully."

"Don't care," he says, crossing his massive arms across his chest. "Spill it or we're going to stand here all night."

My eyes lock with his, but I'm about a thousand percent sure I'm not going to win this staring contest. Sighing, I say, "My dad taught me self-defense—all that stuff I was trying on you in there. Whenever he thought I was getting too cocky, he would lock me up like you just did to highlight the first rule he taught me about fighting men."

"Which was?"

"Strike once hard, put them down, and then get as far away from them as possible."

"That's good advice for self-defense," he says, pausing for a second. "Probably not for life though."

"Seriously? Oh, I really don't need to be psychoanalyzed right now. Really, I don't. May I get in my car, please?"

I try again to reach around him to open the door. I'm not going to be able to move it anyway with him leaning against it. As I start to walk around to the passenger's side, he grabs my arm, immobilizing me with just one hand. I really hate him right now.

"Not yet. Tell me one thing you miss doing with him, and then I'll let you leave." He's holding my arm gently, but firmly, and I have no doubt he will physically restrain me if I try to bolt, so I give in.

"You know you have to go first. Tell me what you miss doing with your mom." It's a stalling technique, but it's worth a try.

He lets go of my arm. "Again, I don't think I agreed to this order, but fine. I miss baking cookies with her."

"Really? You know how to bake cookies?" I say, laughing.

"I knew how to sit and watch her bake cookies, and sample them when they came out of the oven. I used to sit at the kitchen table and put them in the little balls on the cookie sheets, and then eat them right when they came out. I burned my tongue more than once."

He stares at me, waiting for me to talk. I really don't want to play this game. I don't want to talk about my dad right now. I'm trying to stall, hoping he will just leave me alone. I know he won't, but I think he senses I need more time.

"I couldn't walk into bakeries for years after she died. If I went into a friend's house, and his mom was baking cookies, I had to leave. If I close my eyes now, I can still smell the house and still hear her humming while she's baking. It hurt like hell at first, but now it feels nice to remember it," he says. "It's your turn, and we're burning daylight here. One thing you miss about him. Let's go."

I close my eyes and take a deep breath. "I miss being in the ocean with him, swimming with him. I haven't been in the ocean since . . ." I'm starting to choke up a little bit, so I stop.

"Yeah, yeah, yeah, since eight years ago when he died, when everything stopped for you, when you quit living."

"Mason, that's really uncalled for." My eyes snap open. I can't believe what a dick he's being.

"It's not. It's real, Millie. He isn't here anymore, but you are. You can't just quit living." He grabs my arm again and starts pulling me toward his truck. "C'mon, we're going swimming in the ocean right now."

I pull my arm away. "No, we're not. Quit being such an ass. I don't want to go swimming right now."

"We go swimming, and I leave you alone. You said you needed a workout, so let's go."

"You keep saying you'll leave me alone, but you never do."

"Do you want to test how persistent I am? Or do you just want to go for a swim?"

"I haven't done an open-water swim in—" I stop myself from saying eight years, so he won't jump down my throat again. "I'm not in that kind of shape anymore."

"I'm going to swim with you. You know, I'm pretty good

at it. You might even say I do it for a living. I'll be there. You won't drown."

Actually, I kind of want to go swimming now that he's talking about it. It's really hot, and it sounds refreshing. I don't want him to know he's right though. It's the principle of the matter. Raine told me he's almost always right, but he definitely doesn't need to hear that from me right now.

"Fine. If you will finally get off my ass, we can go swimming. I just need to grab my swimsuit from the hotel."

"I'll follow you there," he says. "And, Millie, I'm trained in tactical vehicle intervention. If you try to lose me, I will forcibly stop your car, and extract you on the spot."

When I get out of my car at the hotel, he gets out of his truck and leans against it with his arms folded over his chest.

"I'm assuming if I don't come out of my room you're going to breach the door," I say, rolling my eyes.

"I mean, yeah, I don't want to ruin your security deposit, but if I have to," he says, smiling in a smug way that makes my heart start racing.

I change quickly into my suit and throw a sundress over it. He's still leaning against his truck when I come out of the room. His eyes don't leave me as I walk over to him.

He suggests I ride with him. He opens my door, and puts out his hand to help me up to my seat. Against my better judgment, I take it. A wave of electricity passes from his hand through my body. I knew it would, and it pisses me off.

"Passenger side always picks the music," he says as he climbs in.

"I need something to energize me. Like some kind of old rock."

"Excellent choice." He clicks a few buttons until a classic rock station comes up.

'Layla' comes pouring out of the speakers. I flip my head around and look at him accusingly.

"Oh, c'mon, you planned that."

He laughs. "You know, I actually didn't, but the universe is clearly on my side. Do you want me to change it?"

"No, it's fine. Let it play. I really do like this song."

I lay my head back on the seat and close my eyes. I can see my dad and feel him all around me, and for the first time since he died, it doesn't feel like a knife is stabbing me directly in the heart.

Chapter Twenty

MASON, VIRGINIA BEACH, VIRGINIA, 2019

The minute she takes off her sundress to reveal her swimsuit underneath, I start thinking that swimming might have been a bad idea. Yeah, I'm going to keep my hands off of her, but damn. Just damn. And I thought her workout gear was dangerous.

She's wearing a sleeveless, front-zip rash guard suit. It's fucking sexy to me that she knows what to wear to swim in the ocean. Most women I know would show up in the stringiest bikini and be worthless the first second a wave hit them. I reach in the back of the truck, pull over my swim chest, and get some fins and face masks out.

"Seriously, you drive around with fins and masks in your truck." She looks at me like this is a weird thing.

"Millie, I'm a SEAL. Swimming is literally what I do for a living, among other things. It's like you carrying your computer around. This is my gear."

"It's not like that at all," she says, shaking her head. "Besides, your stuff is going to be way too big for me."

"I carry all sizes, just in case."

"Just in case what?" I can almost see the wheels spinning faster in her brain. "Oh my God, is this one of your moves with the ladies? You take them swimming, and show off your prowess?"

"This is not one of my moves." Believe me, it doesn't take this much.

"I mean, I know you're not making a move on me, but do you do this with the Frog Hogs?"

I jerk my head back. "Where did you hear that term? Don't say that." It sounds so weird coming out of her mouth. I don't want her associated with that side of my life.

"Why? Is it insulting to you?" she says tilting her head and smiling. She has a way of looking at me that makes my heart rate sky-rocket.

"It's insulting to anyone who uses it," I say, looking away. "And, frankly, I wouldn't waste this much energy on them."

"Ha! So you do use this move, but just on the ladies that require a little more work."

There are no ladies that require work around here. Except for you, Millie. Except for you.

"I have all sizes of swim gear, so when my niece and nephews come to visit me, I have some for them."

"Damn, I gave you way too long to come up with an alternative story. I think Virginia Beach is making my interrogation skills soft," she says, sighing.

I hand her the small fins and face mask, and shut the wagon gate. "Can we can just get in the water? Please."

She starts out swimming ahead of me. I can tell her dad trained her—impressive form, a lot of strength. She's handling the swells the right way. But after about fifteen minutes, she starts to slow down. I grab her foot to stop her. I need to check her breathing.

"You okay?" I reach over to take off her mask. She's breathing too hard.

"Uh, I think. I'm really not in this kind of shape anymore." She's struggling for words. Time for a rest.

I grab her arm and pull her toward me. "Here, stop paddling and just rest for a second."

I put my arms under hers and pull her on top of my body, as I lay back to float. She's still struggling.

"C'mon. Rest back," I say firmly, holding her on top of my chest.

"Why do I never have a choice in anything?" She starts to relax as she feels the steadiness of my body below her.

"Because you would choose incorrectly. Stop talking. Just close your eyes and try to breathe normally." I loosen my grip on her, and let her rest on top of me. Her breathing slows down a little bit.

"I think I'm okay now." She tries to slide off of me. I block her with my arm.

"Your breathing's still accelerated. Just rest a little bit more before we head back."

"How do you know my breathing's accelerated?"

"Because you're literally lying on top of me. I can feel every one of your breaths. Quit trying to control everything and just relax."

"Oh my God, Mason," she says, laughing. "Me quit trying to control everything? Are you serious?"

"Shhh, be quiet. You need to save your breath." I playfully put my hand over her mouth. She bites my finger. Damn, I love a sassy woman. She relaxes her head back on my chest.

I see a pod of dolphins swimming to the left of us. I tap her and point. She tenses up a bit when she sees the fins.

"Dolphins, not sharks," I whisper. "We'll let them pass and then head back."

I lay there—floating in the ocean—with my arms wrapped around her and her body lying on top of mine. We silently watch the dolphins bob through the water. I could stay like this forever. It's the most relaxed I've been in decades.

After the dolphins pass, she says, "I think I'm good."

I let her roll off of me. "Okay, try to let the waves take you in a bit. And tap me if you need me to help."

She nods and takes off for the shore. I can tell she's still struggling a bit, but it's easier going this way. She's letting the water carry her a little bit. When we get to shallow-enough water, I grab her waist and stand her up.

"Nice job. You did a little over a mile."

"A little over a mile? That's all we did? I seriously feel like I just swam twenty miles," she says. "That's a lot harder than I remember."

She's breathing hard again—her chest rising and falling. The zipper on her suit has come down a little. I'm doing everything I can not to look at her stunningly perfect breasts. "Well, after all this time, you did great. I'm sure your dad is proud of you."

"Is proud of me? Like he's watching me right now?" She looks up at the sky like she might see his face.

"Sure, why not? You don't think he watches over you?"

"I don't know," she says, still looking at the sky. "But, I do know if he's looking down right now, he's really pissed that I'm hanging out with a SEAL. He made y'all strictly off-limits when he saw one of you flirting with me when I was a teenager."

I laugh. "Totally understandable. No one knows you better than one of your own. There's not one of us that's any good for any woman, to be quite honest."

We wade out of the water and get the towels out of my truck. She rolls her hair up in one of them and grabs a surf poncho out of her bag. If I ever doubted she was a beach girl, I'm one hundred percent sure of it now. She throws on the poncho and starts working underneath it to take off her suit.

"Do you want me to turn around?" I don't really want to, but Culver's suddenly in my head again.

"Why? You can't see anything through the poncho. That's what they're for—quick changes."

I know what they're for, and I can't see anything, but just watching her move to take off her suit is making me sweat. When her suit drops down to the ground, it's more than I can take. I grab my towel and head over to put my stuff in the cab. When I get back over to her, she has her sundress on, and seems to have things on underneath it. To tell you the truth, I can't look too closely. I'm still sweating, and things are starting to get uncomfortable in my swim trunks.

"Are you ready?" I say, averting my eyes.

"Yeah." She stuffs everything into her beach bag and hands my towel back to me. "Thanks for the towel."

She's seriously the most low-maintenance woman I've ever met. It's so hot to me. I follow her around the truck and hesitantly give her my hand to help her climb up. The last time she took my hand, I'm surprised the electricity that shot through me didn't singe her.

She's putting her wet, messy curls in a big knot on top of her head when I get in on my side. She finishes and looks at me. "Do you want me to put your hair up, too?"

"It's not that long." It really is. I'm overdue for a haircut by about a month.

"I don't know. It's getting real hippie looking," she says, laughing.

I shake my head to assess the length. Yeah, it's long. "You probably know from your dad. We aren't the best groomers."

"Yeah, he had really deep auburn hair, and for some reason, his hair grew tall instead of long, and his beard was always really spiky. He looked like a devilish Chia Pet." She laughs honestly for the first time since I've met her.

She stops suddenly and looks at me, her eyes wide.

"That's the first thing you've told me about him without me forcing it out of you," I say, knowing what she's thinking.

She smiles and turns toward the window. I put my hand on her leg as I start the car. She doesn't make me move it. It stays there until we get to her hotel. She sits in the truck until I walk around to open her door. I lift her down and position her way closer to me than she needs to be. I just stand there with her between me and the truck.

She looks up at me with those sparkly eyes, those fucking eyes. "Mason, I have a boyfriend."

"I know." It's all I can think to say.

"And, you and I work together. It would be weird."

"I know that, too." I do know that. And, I know Culver would kill me. None of it matters much to me though.

"I should go." She moves a bit, and I let her get around me.

She walks toward her room, and I follow her. She turns around, her eyes questioning me.

"Just making sure you get in safely." I turn around to walk back to my truck.

"Mason," I hear her say quietly behind me. I turn around immediately.

She takes a deep breath. "Thank you for today. I haven't talked about him for such a long time. It wasn't as bad as I thought it would be. It was kind of nice."

I take a few steps back toward her, and put my hands on her shoulders. "Any time you want to talk about him—I mean any time—no matter where I am, you can call me."

She looks up at me, her eyes widening as she takes a deep breath. "I haven't let myself talk about him because I knew once I opened the dam, the water would never stop coming out. I can't have that in my job. But just letting a little bit out at a time doesn't seem so bad. You're the only person I've really opened up to since it happened."

Her eyes start to tear up, so I grab her and hold her tightly to my chest. She lets me. It's the second time today she's rested on my chest, and there's nothing in this world that has ever felt so right. I'm not sure how long we stood like that, but when she finally starts to pull away, I give her one last gentle squeeze and kiss the top of her head.

I walk away backward, still facing her. "I'm not leaving until I hear the door lock behind you. Go."

"You're seriously so bossy." She laughs that honest laugh again. She closes the door, and I hear the deadbolt click.

I shake my head violently to try to get some blood flowing to that area of my body again. God, what is she doing to me?

Chapter Twenty-One

Mack stopped in the house when he arrived in the Outer Banks to give Camille some extra money for Millie to join the local swim club. He was one hundred percent sure they couldn't teach her anything he hadn't already taught her, but her friends were joining, and it seemed important to her. Mack found Camille in the kitchen.

"Hey. Here's that extra money for the Y swim club," he said, tossing the envelope on the table. "Where's Millie?"

"Oh, that child's off feeling sorry for herself somewhere. She's been in a mood for the entire week," Camille said dismissively.

"Millie's never in a bad mood. What's wrong with her?"

"Well first, hormones. They're spreading through her like the plague."

Mack could have done without that information. She was barely thirteen. He had hoped it was way too early for all that.

"And second, some boy's been picking on her at school," Camille said.

Mack snapped back immediately from his thoughts, his face suddenly serious. "What boy? Where? What's his name? Where does he live?"

"There's no need to get all upset. I told her the boy probably likes her. That's how they show it at that age."

"Likes her? She's thirteen. She's way too young for any of that, Camille."

"Well, nevertheless, it's here. I had boys swarming around me pretty regularly by that age."

Mack tried to think back to when he was thirteen. His memory wasn't what it used to be, but he was pretty damn sure he was still only interested in video games and guns at that age.

"I'm going to look for her," Mack said.

"You coddle her, Mack. She needs to develop thicker skin," Camille called after him.

Mack kept walking. He knew Camille was partially right. Millie needed to be physically tough. That's why he had been training her on self-defense and weapons since she was five. But, mental toughness was another thing. Millie was sweet, trusting, and affectionate—qualities Mack had never had until Millie came into his life. He wanted so badly for her to retain that innocence.

Mack knew Millie would be under the lilac bushes, as usual. She had figured out early in her life that Camille was deathly afraid of bees and would never come near that side of the yard in the summer.

"Hey, Mills," Mack said, watching the bees fly peacefully around her.

Of course, she's finally won them over to her side, Mack thought, smiling.

"Hey," she said dejectedly without looking up at him.

"You wanna come out of there?" Mack asked. He didn't much like bees either.

She rolled over and quickly army-crawled out of the bushes. He couldn't help but feel proud of her flawless execution of the techniques he had taught her—head low, butt low, pull yourself through like you're doing chin-ups in the dirt.

She didn't make a move to stand up after she'd cleared the bushes, so he reached down, picked up her defeated body, and hugged it to him. She didn't return the hug, but she didn't pull away either. He let her stand there, her sad, little limp body pressed against him, until he felt his shirt getting wet. He looked down to see her crying silently.

"Come here, Mills," he said, guiding her over to the wall of the house. They both sat down with their backs to it, his arm around her and her head resting on his shoulder.

"Camille said some boy's been picking on you."

"Yeah," she said quietly.

"Who is he? What's his name?"

"I'm not going to tell you his name," Millie said.

"Why?"

"Because he's a mean jerk, but I don't want him dead."

Mack smiled. She'd been able to read his mind since she was just a little girl.

"Well, why don't you tell me about it? What did he say?

Did he touch you?" Mack asked, trying to keep his anger under control.

She nuzzled more closely into him. Mack had heard one of the guys at work talking about how his teenage daughter no longer wanted him to hug her. Mack had been dreading that day with Millie. He hugged her tightly, thankful that day hadn't come yet.

"He didn't touch me," she said through her sniffles. "He just told me I was ugly."

A fire ignited within Mack. The exact same fire he felt right before a firefight. He wanted to hunt this kid down, and beat the crap out of him. He took a deep breath and forced himself to calm down.

"Millie, you're the most beautiful girl on earth. You know that."

"You think I am, but that's just because you're my dad," she said. "All the other girls are wearing makeup, but Camille says I'm too young for that."

Mack was stunned that he finally agreed with Camille on something.

"Millie, if I showed you two presents—one with colorful wrapping paper and a big, flashy bow and one in a plain box— and then I told you the one with all the wrapping had nothing inside, but the one in the plain box was full of amazing presents, which one would you choose?"

"So, you're telling me I'm the plain box without any wrapping?"

Mack smiled. He knew she had always been too quick for her own good.

"I'm telling you you're the box full of amazing presents.

The box that took the time to fill up with all the good things before it got all wrapped up. When you're older, you can wrap yourself up in makeup, and whatever else you want, and then everyone is going to be jealous that the box with the most amazing presents inside is also wrapped the most beautifully."

She lifted her head to look at him. "But for now, I'm plain like the box."

"Sweetie, there is nothing plain about you. You're the most beautiful girl in the world, inside and out. And if that boy doesn't see it, he doesn't even deserve to look at you," Mack said, still trying to figure out a way to learn the boy's identity.

She laid her head back down on him and sighed. "I want to start wrapping my box now."

"There's plenty of time for all that, Mills. Just enjoy still being a kid. Keep filling up your box. That other stuff will come with time."

Mack took a deep breath, suddenly knowing she had already passed through the kid phase and was quickly, too quickly, approaching the young woman phase—full of its heartbreak that he couldn't shield her from. He wanted to stop it like an approaching enemy force, just point his rifle at it, and start firing. *If only it were that easy*, he thought.

Chapter Twenty-Two

It's late in the afternoon, and I haven't seen Mason all day. I've kept myself locked down in Raine's office, trying desperately to find Haroun Hadzic's house. I'm just about to close my computer and head back to the hotel when Mason walks in.

"So, any new leads on Hadzic's father?"

I'm a little thrown just by the sight of him after being up all night thinking about floating on his chest in the ocean. He stares at me, all business, like nothing happened yesterday.

"Um, m-maybe," I stutter. "I've been going over the area Petrovic told me about for days, but I haven't seen anything that looks like what he described. Culver put me in touch with an Air Force captain in Afghanistan. He's had his guys do some runs over the area to see if they can see anything that I'm missing on the satellite. I'm waiting for him to get back to me today."

"What happens if he doesn't find anything?"

"Well, I'll keep looking, but from D.C. There's not much reason for me to be down here if I don't have anything for you guys to do."

All of a sudden he looks pissed, like I've said something wrong.

"So, just back to the D.C. life?"

"Yeah, I mean, I guess. That's where I live."

"Back to the boyfriend?"

The question takes me by surprise. "We haven't talked in a few weeks, since I've been down here, but yeah, we're still dating."

"You haven't talked to him at all since you've been down here? You haven't missed him? That doesn't seem like much of a relationship." His voice is demanding answers that my brain just can't give him right now.

"I didn't say I didn't miss him." I don't, but technically I didn't say that.

"Do you?" He's staring right at me, challenging me to tell him the truth. He knows I have feelings for him, too. I shrug and try to concentrate on my computer.

"I don't know, Millie. It seems like you deserve something a little more passionate than that."

"Why are we even talking about this? It's not really any of your business. No offense, but it's not."

He stands up suddenly. "You're right. It's not. Let me know what the Air Force finds."

And just like that, he walks out of the office, leaving me confused and more than a little disappointed.

I know he's right about Drew and me. Despite Drew's many calls and texts, I haven't talked to him since I left for

Virginia Beach. I always call him at least every couple days when I travel, but now, it's been almost two weeks. There are many reasons for that, but it's at least partially because of the feelings I'm starting to have for Mason. That's another problem I'm going to have to take care of, but one step at a time. I know the first thing I have to do is break up with Drew.

When I get back to my hotel room, I down a couple glasses of wine, and then call Drew. He picks the call up on the first ring.

"Oh my God, she's alive."

"Hey. Sorry, it's been a crazy few weeks."

"Are you okay? I was really worried about you."

"Yeah, I'm fine," I say. "Hey, Drew, we need to talk. I don't want to do this over the phone, but you deserve an answer."

"An answer to what?" Drew asks slowly.

"An answer to why I haven't been calling you."

"I just figured you were busy," he says. "Is there more to it than that?"

"Yeah, Drew, there is. I'm sorry to do this over the phone."

"Wait, are you breaking up with me?"

I close my eyes and dive in. "I think it's best if we break up. I'm sorry. I love you, but it's not working out for me."

He doesn't say anything, but I still hear him breathing. I'll let him have a moment.

"Millie, God, I don't even know what you're talking about. We've been dating for two years, and you're just going to call me and break up with me? Where are you? I'll come there, but we can't have this conversation on the phone. Is there somebody else?"

"There's not anyone else," I say, lying slightly. "It's just my job. It's only going to get busier, and it's not fair to you."

"Don't use that excuse," Drew says with anger creeping into his voice. "I've never complained once about your travel schedule. If you want to break up with me, tell me why you want out of the relationship, not why you think I do."

"I don't know . . . It's just not a priority for me, and after two years, I think it should be."

"It's not a priority for you? Damn, Millie, you just said you love me, but I'm not even a priority. What's wrong with you?"

"I'm not sure," I say. "But you deserve someone who will make you a priority. You're an amazing guy."

"I swear to God if you say, 'It's not you, it's me,' I'm going to lose it," Drew shouts, making me jump. I try to keep my tone steady.

"I'm sorry, Drew. I really am, but I'm not going to change my mind."

There's more silence on the other end of the phone. He finally says, "When are you back in town?"

"I'm not sure, but probably in the next few days. I'll come by and get my stuff whenever it's convenient for you."

"Let's at least have dinner and talk about it a little more. You owe me that. Will you call me when you get back here?"

I agree to call him for dinner. He sounds like he's in agony when he says goodbye. I feel guilty that I'm not. The only thing on my mind right now is Mason. It pisses me off so badly, but my mind won't turn him off. I know he'll be at the bar, and that's where I find my body headed.

I walk in and look around to see if he's there. I don't see

him by the pool tables which is usually where he hangs out, so I decide to just have a drink, and head back to the hotel. I take the same stool I had the first night I came here. After a few minutes, Pete walks over and hands me what looks like a martini.

"I googled how to make a dirty martini," Pete says, smiling proudly.

"What? That's amazing. Thank you." I notice a little redness coming to his cheeks before he quickly turns and walks away.

I take a sip. Way too much olive juice, but Pete made it for me, so I'm drinking all of it. While I'm in deep thought about my drink, two muscular arms snake around me, the hands landing on the bar on either side of me, penning me in. I figure it's Mason or one of the team, so I don't react. But then the body moves closer to me and says, "I'll buy your next round."

I don't recognize the voice. I pull back to look at an unfamiliar face.

"What the fuck? Get off of me," I say, trying to push myself out of his arms.

"Is that any way to say thank you?" the random guy says as he pulls me into a tight squeeze.

I look up to see Pete walking back over.

"Get off her," he says.

"C'mon, I'm just having a little fun, Petey boy."

Pete shrugs and walks away. "It's your funeral, man."

The guy squeezes me tighter again. I push back against his chest while I try to move one of his arms. Nothing moves. Then, I jab one of my elbows into his side, and he flies off me. I'm starting to think I'm a little stronger than I thought when I see Mason pinning my assailant to the bar with one hand. I turn around to see the entire team now crowded around me.

"Whoa, whoa, guys," I say, standing up and trying to push them back a bit. "I've got this."

They don't move. They seriously look like they're about to rip the guy apart.

"Mason," I say, tapping him on his arm to try to break the death grip he has on the guy's throat. "Too much fire power. We're all good here. I've got this."

He looks at me. The ocean-blue eyes have turned steely. "No, I've got this."

He looks back at the guy, gives his throat one more squeeze, and shoves him roughly against the bar as he lets him go. "You need to leave."

The guy has recovered enough to stand upright. He's obviously had a few too many, though, and is feeling a little liquid courage. "Man, why don't you mind your own business? I'm just trying to buy the lady a drink."

"Oh, hell no," Hawk says, taking a gigantic step toward him, and pushing him back against the bar. The entire team moves toward him.

"Guys, seriously, way too much for one drunk idiot. Stand down." I block them about as successfully as a kid trying to guard an entire NBA team.

Mason puts his hand up and they back off immediately. I'm going to have to get him to teach me how to do that. He looks back at the drunk idiot and says with a gravelly tone that I haven't heard before, "She is my business. And, I told you to leave."

The guy seems to finally be sobering up a little bit, at least enough to calculate his odds of being killed in the next few minutes. He starts to walk away. "Yeah, yeah, fine. She's not even that hot anyway."

"I'm not that hot? Seriously? Was that really necessary? Hawk, you can hit him now. Seriously, just go crazy on him."

Hawk smiles and pats me on the shoulder. "I still think you're hot, Mills."

Chapter Twenty-Three

MASON, VIRGINIA BEACH, VIRGINIA, 2019

"You okay?" I pull out a bar stool for her, and then sit down on the one next to her.

"What the hell was that?" She looks at me, her eyes a little wider than usual.

"I knew the guy had no chance with you, so I thought I'd try to save him the rejection."

She shakes her head in amazement, eyes still wide.

"You need another drink?" I ignore her look and motion to Pete.

Pete comes back over. "I tried to warn him, Mase."

"Why didn't you try to warn him about me, Pete? I'm the real ninja here," she says.

"It's true, Pete. I've seen her skills."

Pete's not impressed. "You want another round?"

"Yeah. Whiskey and whatever she's drinking."

"It's called a dirty martini, Mason. Man, get some class," Pete says, smiling as he walks away.

"Seriously, Mason," she says, nudging me on the shoulder. The minute she touches me, I have to physically brace myself on the bar to keep from grabbing her. I want to kiss her so badly right now.

"So, are operators required to have anger issues? Or is that just a happy side effect of the job?" She looks down at my hands tightly gripping the bar.

"Not really required, but usually the case," I say, smiling as I try to loosen my grip.

"Well, let me tell you, you get an A-plus in that area. I mean you really excel at it."

"Well, you know, if you can't be the best at something."

It looks like Pete's a little backed up, so I decide to take matters into my own hands. "Tell me how to make a dirty martini."

"Well, first, Pete makes it wrong. He uses way too much olive juice for me. So, a couple to three ounces of vodka, half an ounce of vermouth, and just a little splash of olive juice. He made my first one way too salty."

"So mainly vodka with more sweet than salty?"

"Exactly."

I walk around the bar and start finding the ingredients.

"So, you can just go back there and make drinks?"

"It wouldn't be the first time." I look over my shoulder. "Pete, I've got her drink."

"Mason, you don't have to—I can wait."

"I know I don't have to, Millie. I want to. That's why I offered."

I turn my baseball hat backward, and rub my hands

together. I feel like I'm about to disarm a bomb. I pour three healthy shots of vodka, and add the rest.

"Your dirty martini, ma'am," I say, bowing to her.

She takes a long drink and smiles at me. "You've done this before. It's perfect."

"Like I said, if you can't be the best at something."

"So, did you tell them about my dad being a SEAL?" She gestures over to my team.

"No. I told you I wouldn't, and I won't."

"It's just the way they reacted when the guy was hitting on me. . . It felt personal."

"It was personal. I keep telling you that you're part of the family now. Maybe you'll believe me one day."

"That was something my dad told me, too. That if anything ever happened to him, his team would take care of me."

"And did they?"

"Yeah, they tried. I didn't really let them."

"You? Resisting someone's help? Get out of here," I say, rolling my eyes.

"I always think I can take care of myself. I had this boyfriend in high school. He kind of bothered me after I broke up with him. I told him off, and he never looked at me again. I was feeling like a badass, and then I found out that Dad had come to school and threatened the guy, and literally made him pee in his pants. I never knew that until after Dad died."

"That's amazing. If I ever had a daughter, I would do the exact same thing. You know, Mills, I know you've felt like a lone wolf since your dad died, but that's not healthy. You need a team, some backup. It doesn't matter where you are—you're part of us now. We have your back."

"Yeah, I guess. I'm just not used to relying on other people. Except for my dad and, you know, when he died, I just thought I'd be better on my own, calling my own shots."

"I think you're looking at having a team the wrong way," I say, turning my body to fully face her. "The important part is choosing your team members correctly. Everyone of my teammates is as strong as I am. When we're on a mission, if I get in a tight spot, the next person has my back until I can get right again. Then when he gets in a tight spot, I have his back until he gets right. It's not that I'm better than him or he's better than me. We have the exact same skill set—it's just a timing thing. When I get backwards, he has me, and vice versa. It's fluid. Like when we enter a target, guys peel off left and right to clear what needs to be cleared, and the next person in line just takes over the lead. It's not that the person in front of you can't lead anymore. It's just that they've taken a detour to do what they need to do, so you pick up where they left off. No one can lead a hundred percent of the time. You need other people in your corner who can pick up when you need help. You just have to make sure that they're as good at it as you are."

"Yeah, but who's as good at taking care of me as I am?"

"Your dad was," I say slowly, not wanting to spook her too much. "And, if you'll let me in, I could be, too. Let me fight some of your battles for you."

"I don't think you take care of all of your teammates quite like the way you just took care of me," she says, laughing.

"For instance, I don't think you would intervene like that if the guy was hitting on Butch."

"If that guy was hitting on Butch, the only thing I'd be doing is fitting him for a body bag."

She laughs again, her eyes sparkling at me. "Maybe you should start thinking of me as one of the guys. Like I'm Butch."

I sigh. I think I've pushed her hard enough for tonight. I put my hand on her thigh as I stand up. "I'll be honest, Mills. If I thought about Butch the way I'm thinking about you right now, I'm the one who would need a body bag."

I slam the rest of my whiskey, look at her one last time, and force myself to walk back over to where the guys are playing darts. By the time I look back for her, she's gone. For the best. She's still resisting, and I need to stop pushing her. That can only end badly for both of us. But I already know I'm going to be wide awake all night thinking of her. Like every night since she first walked into my life.

Chapter Twenty-Four

OUTER BANKS, NORTH CAROLINA, 2010

Mack listened to Millie's voicemail as soon as he got back from training. She was sobbing, but he had been able to make out that she had broken up with the Rob kid she was dating. It was the last part of the message that made him head directly to his car to drive down to the Outer Banks.

Millie said Rob wouldn't leave her alone—that he was stalking her. Mack had learned as Millie got deeper into her teen years that she was getting more dramatic with her language. But the sound of her crying, combined with use of the word "stalker," lit a fire in Mack that he knew couldn't be put out until he had a talk with this boy.

"You're going to North Carolina? You know we only have a couple days before deployment," Chase said, walking quickly behind Mack through the parking lot.

"Yeah, Millie left me a voicemail. Some boy's been harassing her. I'm gonna work that out before we leave," Mack said.

"Work it out? Yeah, how about I come down there with you, and monitor how this gets worked out before I have to pull your ass out of jail." Chase grabbed Mack's shoulder to stop him.

"No, man, I'm good. I'm good. Just need to have a little talk with him," Mack said, shrugging off Chase's hand.

Chase saw the gun outline under Mack's T-shirt. "Why don't you leave the weapons here then? I'll hold on to your gun for you."

Chase held out his hand. Mack begrudgingly handed him the gun.

"Maybe give me the knife, too," Chase said, knowing there was at least one knife somewhere on Mack's body.

"Ah, brother, I'm not going without my knife. You never know when you're going to need to cut a bagel or something," Mack said, getting into his truck.

"We need you on this deployment, dumbass. Try not to kill anyone," Chase said, sighing as he turned back toward his own car.

As Mack drove down to the Outer Banks, he thought about the last couple times he had been with Millie. Even grown men were stopping in their tracks to admire her. It made Mack want to have a talk with all of them individually, but for now, a talk with Rob would do.

Although Millie had been dating Rob for about six months, Mack hadn't met him yet. Rob was suspiciously unavailable every time Mack was in town. He'd thought for a while that Millie was making the boyfriend up. Actually, he was hoping it. He still thought Millie was too young to be dating. But, his friend Carol had confirmed that Rob existed, and that he and Millie were an item. She told Mack that Rob was a nice young man from a good family. Mack had always had doubts, and this was confirming it.

Mack drove into town around noon. It was lunch-time at the school. The kids were eating at the tables outside when he arrived. He grabbed a kid who was walking through the parking lot, and gave him twenty dollars to point out which one Rob was. The kid gladly gave up the information. Mack had a feeling no one really liked this Rob kid.

Mack watched Rob from his truck. The kid was pretending to talk to his friends, but his head kept turning around to look at Millie's table. *I see you, kid. Just keep looking at her, and we'll see what happens,* Mack thought.

Rob made his way over to Millie's table. He snuck up behind her and put his hands on her shoulders. Millie tried to shake his hands off, but Rob kept them firmly planted. Mack knew that Millie could take the kid down, and he wondered why she didn't.

"Leave me alone!" Millie finally screamed as she stood up, and walked away. Mack hadn't heard that tone in her voice before. She sounded scared, and that made every hair on his body stand on end.

He watched as Rob smiled at her and walked away. He knew he didn't have the slightest intention of leaving her alone. Mack snuck in the school through the side entrance, just in time to see Rob entering the bathroom. He followed him in, locked the door, and used the door stop to barricade them in.

As he was standing at the urinal, Rob heard the door lock. He looked over and saw it was closed, but didn't see anyone. He returned to his business. He was unzipping when he felt something on his neck. He whipped around—still exposed—to see Mack standing in front of him. He gasped at the sight of him. Rob hadn't heard him approaching, and now this danger-ous-looking man was standing six inches from his face.

"Sorry, man, I didn't see you," Rob said quickly, his voice cracking.

Rob tried to step around him. Mack moved his leg to block Rob's exit. Mack didn't say anything. Rob moved quickly backward, almost falling into the urinal. Mack smiled and pulled an apple out of his pocket. He started peeling it with the knife he pulled out of his waist-band. He peeled the apple so precisely that the thin scraps were slowly floating to the ground like little red kites.

Without looking up from the apple, Mack said quietly, "Millie is off-limits to you from this moment on. You don't look at her. You don't talk to her. You don't get near her. You understand that?"

Mack looked up, his eyes almost searing a hole into Rob's forehead. Rob stood as still as a statue, stunned into silence. His eyes started watering and sweat began dripping from his forehead. He finally nodded vigorously, still not able to speak. Mack reached over and wiped both sides of his knife clean on Rob's shirt. As Mack walked slowly away, Rob's bladder emptied involuntarily onto the bathroom floor.

Mack headed to the school office. The secretary hesitated when he said he'd like to take Millie out of school for the afternoon. He didn't blame her. He knew he didn't look much like the other dads. She called for Millie over the PA.

"Dad, what are you doing here?" Millie came flying into the office, and jumped into Mack's arms. "Are you okay?"

"Yeah, sweetie, I'm fine. I just wanted to see you one more time before I left on deployment," Mack said. "I have a few hours. Do you want to go down to the beach?"

"Like instead of being in school?" Millie asked. "Um, of course."

Mack signed her out with the still-dubious secretary. They headed down to the beach with Millie jabbering all the way.

"Dad, did you get the message I left you? I broke up with Rob, and he was being an idiot, like following me around, and stuff. But, it's weird. Like just ten minutes ago, I passed him in the hall when I was coming to the office to see you, and he wouldn't even look at me. Like, he literally ran into a locker to get away from me. Isn't that weird?"

"Yeah, that's weird," Mack said, smiling. "Maybe he figured out what a badass you are, and he doesn't want to mess with you anymore."

"Probably," Millie said as they pulled into the parking lot at the public beach access. They walked hand-in-hand to the sea wall. For a few minutes, they watched silently as the high tide crashed against the wall.

"Hey, Mills, I want to tell you more about your mom," Mack said slowly.

"More? You've barely told me anything."

"That was a mistake. I should have."

"Camille told me that I was the result of a one-night stand," Millie said, looking up at Mack.

"What did I tell you about what Camille says?"

"That it's mainly bullshit."

"It's ALL bullshit," Mack said. "You weren't the result of a one-night stand. I worked with your mom. We knew each other for a while before . . . Well, before we became intimate."

"What happened? Why did you stop dating?"

"Mills, we weren't really dating. I liked her. I respected her. But we only worked together for a little bit. You know how my job works. I'm in and out of places so fast."

"So, she got pregnant, and you just moved on?" Millie asked, not believing that Mack would do that.

"Of course not, Millie. You know I would have never done that. I didn't know she was pregnant until after she already had you. She didn't tell me. I don't know why. Maybe she tried. You know I'm hard to reach when I'm working. I really don't know what happened."

"But, she died when she was having me?"

"Right after, yeah," Mack said.

"How did you know about me?"

"One of her friends called me after you were born. When I found out about you—and found out she had died—I took leave immediately and went to get you."

"In New York, right?"

"Yeah, in New York." Mack still couldn't bring himself to tell her the entire truth.

"Did her parents know about me? Her brothers and sisters?"

"Her parents died before she did, and she was an only child. That's one of the reasons I haven't told you much about her. You don't have any family on that side," Mack said.

"You told me her name was Marie. What was her last name?"

"Miller. Marie Miller." Mack was more prepared with an

answer this time. He had already looked in the New York State obituaries. There were hundreds of Marie Millers listed. If Millie ever went searching for clues about her mom, that would at least slow her down for a while.

"Do you have any pictures of her?"

"No, and I wish I did. When I got to New York, you were already in a foster home. I was concentrated on getting you home. I didn't even take time to try to find her friends. I didn't know any of them."

"Why are you telling me all of this now?"

"Because I want you to know that I respected your mom," Mack said. "I liked her, and if we had had more time together, I might have even loved her. It wasn't a one-night stand. She was way too precious for that. I'm telling you this now because I want you to know you are way too precious to be disrespected in any way by anyone, especially by men. You don't have to do anything you don't want to do. And, you shouldn't do anything that you're uncomfortable with."

"Dad, I haven't had sex yet. You can take a deep breath," Millie said, patting Mack's arm.

Mack took a minute to take that breath. "Was this boy, this Rob kid, trying to force you?"

"Not force. I mean, that's why I broke up with him because he wanted to have sex, and I didn't want to, but he wasn't trying to force me."

"Millie, if a guy ever tries to force you to do anything you don't want to do, I don't care how old you are," Mack said, pausing to let the anger from the mere thought of it subside slightly. "Well, first, you tell me, so I can kill him, and then you break up with him."

"Do you think it might make more sense for me to break up with him first, and then you kill him?" Millie said, laughing.

"Not necessarily. Either way, he's going to die," Mack said. "And, I still think you should carry a gun."

"I don't need a gun, Dad. I don't want one. We've talked about that."

"Well, we can keep talking about it, but I definitely think you should consider it. You handle guns as well as I did at your age. I would trust you with one."

"Dad," Millie sighed dramatically.

"And Millie, if I'm ever not around, I want you to know you have a family outside of Camille. All my teammates, my brothers, will take care of you if I can't."

"What do you mean if you're not around? Are you going somewhere?" Millie asked, concern starting to creep onto her face.

Mack could tell he'd gone too far. "No, sweetie. I'm not going anywhere. I'll always be here for you."

Chapter Twenty-Five

Thankfully, I've had almost no time to think about the way Mason and I left things at the bar. I had barely gotten back to my hotel room last night when I had a call from my counterpart in Afghanistan. He told me the Air Force thought they'd found Haroun Hadzic's house. They located a shack, half built into the mountain, in the area Petrovic described to me. One of our Afghan agents confirmed with the locals that the man living there is called Hadzic.

So this morning, we're already wheels up to Afghanistan to pay Haroun Hadzic a visit. After much deliberation, I finally convinced Culver I need to go with the team to interview Hadzic at his house. The intel suggests he's incapacitated. The locals told our agent he's very sick, and he can no longer walk very well.

Mason does not want me on the mission, and I can understand why. But, I finally convinced Culver that Hadzic won't make the trip up the mountain to the extraction helicopter even if he was carried.

Honestly, I don't much want to go on the mission. I mean, I'm in good shape, and I can shoot a gun, but these guys are elite warriors, and I don't want to get in their way. But Hadzic is the closest I have ever been to Sayid Custovic, and I'm not willing to risk him dying in transit back to the base.

The team's starting to gear up, so I head over to them to get ready, although I don't really know what that means.

"Should I carry a gun?" I say as I approach them.

The guys start laughing, shaking their heads.

"No," Mason says firmly. "No."

This is the first time he's looked at me directly today, and he has absolutely none of the gentleness in his eyes that I saw last night.

"I know how to handle a gun. I'm a pretty decent shot."

"You're a good shot on the firing range. It's different," JJ says without looking up at me.

Mason looks at me to see if I'm going to drop it. The expression on my face must say no. He walks over to me, staring at me intensely.

"Have you ever shot someone?"

I've never even pointed a gun at someone.

He reads my mind. "That's why you don't get a gun."

"But, if something happens—"

"You see this gun?" He gestures forcefully toward his pistol. "We all have them. If every one of us dies on this mission, and you're still living, then you have my permission to take one of our guns and shoot the hell out of anyone and everyone you see, but while any of us are still living, you don't touch a gun. You got that?"

"Yes, sir," I reply, looking for any of that humor I've become accustomed to seeing in his face. None of it is there.

"Don't call me sir," he says brusquely. "Mouse, get her in her vest and helmet."

Mouse pulls me away. He fastens my vest around me and tightens the straps. I feel like a little kid being dressed for school. I grab my helmet and start to put it on. Mouse intercepts and starts securing for me.

"It's important that you get the gear on the right way or it's not going to do you any good. Let me do it for you. It takes a while to get a hang of this stuff." Mouse is smiling sweetly, like he's tying my ice skates before we head out for a day on the pond.

"I don't get night-vision goggles?" I ask quietly, noticing that my helmet is the only one without them.

"It takes a while to figure out the goggles. You'll be in between two of us. Just do what we do, go where we go. You'll be fine."

The pilot announces the landing. We buckle in. The minute the wheels hit the ground, the guys are up, heading toward the cargo door. I guess I'm supposed to do that, too. I head that way, struggling to keep my balance as the pilot brakes the plane hard. The guys are standing so easily, it looks like they're just casually riding a wave into the beach.

The cargo door opens. The guys head down the ramp. I feel someone pushing me from behind. It's Bryce. He's not looking at me. I start running down the ramp to keep up with their monster strides.

The helicopter's there, blades turning, ready to take off. The guys start piling in. Someone lifts me from behind and basically throws me to Hawk, who grabs my vest and pulls me through the guys until I'm sitting safely in the middle of the helicopter. The guys are sitting with their backs to me, legs dangling out the open doors with their guns at the ready.

The helicopter lifts off and starts weaving its way through the mountains. I'm pretty strong, but I'm having a problem just sitting upright when the pilot starts swerving through the passes. The guys are just sitting there, hanging half-way out of the helicopter, looking like they're taking a Sunday drive.

The pilot does some crazy landing, and with the skids barely touching the ground, someone pulls me off. The guys are on full alert now. Everything's quiet except the sound of the helicopter flying away in the background.

Mason gets down in my face. "You're between Hawk and Mouse. Do exactly what they do. They stop. You stop. They squat down. You squat down. Don't talk, and keep up."

I haven't seen his face look like this before. I nod. We fall out into a half run. Mouse taps me as he starts, and I follow. We start descending. It's rocky and slippery. I'm looking side to side to get my bearings. I can't see anything.

Hawk stills my head with one hand. "Forward," he commands, and I obey.

I just focus on Mouse's back. When it slows down, I slow down. When it speeds up, I speed up. It starts to feel more routine as we progress. We stop a few times. They look around. I don't. I'm focused on Mouse's back.

In what seems like a half an hour or so, we come to a full stop. The guys are spread out, looking over a ridge. Hawk pushes me down by his feet. I stay there. They're all looking through their scopes, scanning back and forth.

"Bryce, Butch, go," Mason orders.

They spring up, and disappear around the ridge. Hawk has me pressed up against the ridge with his leg, so I'm not going anywhere. I stay quiet and listen. I don't hear anything, not even Bryce and Butch moving. It's just dead silent.

After a few minutes, I hear Mason say, "Roger that. We're headed that way."

Hawk's leg releases me as he pulls me up. I guess we're moving again. I see Mouse move, and I follow. We wind down the path for a few more minutes. I don't even see the house until we're right on top of it. Well, it's really not a house. It's more like a cave.

Mason grabs me and pulls me toward the front door. Mouse and Hawk stay outside. I enter to see Bryce and Butch standing with an old man seated on a chair in between them. There's an empty chair facing the old man.

"You've got ten minutes," Mason says as I sit down.

The man's eyes are just barely visible on his unbelievably wrinkled face. I'm not sure he's even alive until he spits at me.

Butch slaps the back of his head. "Show some manners, old man."

"Butch." I shake my head at him, and he straightens up.

"Mr. Hadzic, we don't have much time," I say in Bosnian. "So I'll get right to it. I know your son, Yusef, works for Sayid Custovic. And, I know Yusef visits you here periodically. I know where your daughters live in Sarajevo. I know where your grandchildren go to school. All I need to know from you is where I can find Yusef when he's not visiting you. And then we'll leave you here."

He spits at me again. Or at least tries to. He's so damn old. I don't even know if he has any saliva left. Butch wants to back-hand him again. I shoot him a side eye, and he pulls his hand back.

"I saw your granddaughter playing last week at school. What is she, about eight now? Have you seen her lately? She's very pretty. She looks just like her mother. I guess they can't really get out here to see their grandfather though. Too bad. I'm going to see them soon. I'll tell them hello if you want me to."

He tries to lean toward me and almost falls out of the chair. Bryce grabs his shoulder and pulls him back into the chair a little too roughly.

"Tell me where I can find Yusef or I'll have these men take your daughters in and ask them where he is. Believe me you don't want these men touching your daughters."

He squints so severely that it looks like his face is melting.

"I don't know where my son is. Yusef is dead to me," he finally manages to say.

"Really? Because we know he moved you here. I'm guessing at your request. You always were a supporter of the radicals. You just need to be close to the action, right? You can't walk anymore, so you can't really be in the fight, but I'm sure you get your fix when Yusef visits and tells you all about the Americans he's killing."

"You are a whore," he says in very broken English, pronouncing whore as "who-ruh."

"Yes, I am," I reply in English. "I fucked all of these men

to get them to bring me here, and I'm going to do it again when we leave."

Well, at least I know Bryce and Butch are paying attention now.

"Tell me where I can find Yusef," I continue in Bosnian. "Or I will have these men drag you up that mountain, and you will come back to the United States with us, where you will die in the land of the whores."

He blinks. I think it is the first time he has blinked this entire conversation. Again, I wasn't even sure his eyelids were working, but he blinked. He's done. I don't know if he really believes we're going to drag his old ass up that mountain, but he's not going to take the chance.

I stand up and look at Butch. "Grab him," I say in Bosnian, knowing that Butch can't understand me. "He's coming back with us."

"Wait," the old man says immediately.

I take a step closer to him. He cringes at the whore standing so close to him.

"I don't know where he lives. He never says. But he goes back to Sarajevo every month or so. I believe he's there now."

"When was Yusef last here?"

"He was just here a few days ago."

I look around the room. I see a few pieces of fruit and bread on the counter. They look fairly fresh. He's probably telling the truth.

I look at Mason across the room. "We're done," I say as I walk toward him.

"What do you want us to do about him?" Mason asks.

"Well, he can't walk, so he's not going to tell anyone until

Yusef visits next, and hopefully, we'll have Yusef by then. And, he probably doesn't have a phone."

"No phone," Bryce says from behind me.

Of course, they cleared and searched the room before I got here. I forget how thorough these guys are.

"So we just leave him?" Mason says.

"We just leave him."

As I walk away, the old man says in Bosnian, "You look just like her. She was a whore, too." I try to recover quickly, but he can see that he surprised me, and that makes him smile.

"You will burn in hell just like she did," he says.

I turn around toward the door, a knot forming rapidly in my stomach. "Probably," I say without looking back. "I'll see you there."

I need to collect my thoughts for a second, but we start immediately back up the mountain. We're doing double time. My quads are sore, and I'm so thirsty, but Mouse's back is still moving, so I'm still moving. The guys seem a little more wound up than usual. I didn't know that was even possible. But their usual hyper alert is on overdrive.

"Roger that," I hear Mason say from somewhere behind me. I don't have a headset on, so I can't hear what they hear. Just the replies.

"That ridge." Mason points to a place just above us. "Hawk, take her."

What's going on? Is the helicopter meeting us somewhere else? I know we've only been climbing for about fifteen minutes. We can't be at the original landing zone yet. Hawk grabs my vest and half pulls and half lifts me to the ridge, and shoves me down behind it. He squats down beside me. "Stay down. And when I say move, you move."

My eyes must have said yes because he stands back up and rests his rifle on the ridge while his leg forcefully pins me against the rocks. I suddenly hear a loud bang, and then all hell breaks loose. It sounds like fireworks are exploding all around me. Not up in the sky, but right beside me. The sound is deafening. Rocks fall on my head. Dust swirls violently around me. I feel like I've suddenly been swept up into the eye of a tornado.

Hawk's leg is vibrating against me as he fires his gun, slamming me into the rocks repetitively. Something hits my head hard. The pain surges through me like someone stabbed me. I think I hear myself yelp through the noise that suffocates me. Curling into a ball against the wall, I cover my head and start rocking back and forth. Everything is exploding and vibrating around me. Suddenly, Hawk yanks me up by my vest.

"Move!" he shouts as he throws me up the path.

Somehow, Mouse is in front of me again, or someone is, and we are triple-timing it up the mountain. My adrenaline has suddenly made all the soreness and pain in my body go away. I feel like I could run at this pace for days. We keep climbing.

The guys are yelling and the guns keep firing on us from behind. I'm not fully registering what's happening. I feel like I'm watching it from above. I just concentrate on the body in front of me. It's still moving, so I'm still moving. As we round yet another switchback, I suddenly see the helicopter landing in a valley ahead of us.

The guys pick up the speed. It's too much for me. I feel

myself falling. I'm headed for the ground when I feel Hawk grab me and throw me over his shoulder without breaking his stride. The helicopter blades are so loud. I feel like they're inches from me. Hawk shields my head with his massive hand and passes me off to Mason like he's a quarterback handing the football off to his running back.

Mason pulls me into the helicopter. He has me between his legs with my back resting on his chest. One of his arms is around me, and the other is pushing my head away from the guns that are still firing at us. The rest of the guys are firing back. As we get higher and higher into the sky, the guns fade off into the background, and everything goes quiet.

I really don't remember the helicopter landing or walking to the transport. Or if I even did walk on my own. But here I am, sitting on a bench, strapped in and ready for takeoff. I look around. The guys are all up, taking off their gear. We must already be in the air. I look down at myself. My protective vest is already off. My helmet's gone. I don't remember taking it off. My head's hazy, and my eyes feel like they're leaking. I reach up to wipe my face and pull my hand away to see blood. Somehow, it doesn't surprise me. Shock, I realize. I think I'm in shock. I've seen it happen to people. It happened to me when my dad died. I think this is what it felt like. I can't remember.

I'm staring at the blood on my hand when Mason suddenly appears. He kneels in front of me. "Hey. You okay? Here. Look at me. Look right in my eyes. That's good. Now breathe. You're okay. Just breathe." He's talking so fast.

"Ty!" I hear him yell.

Then Ty's kneeling in front of me, too.

"She's in shock," Mason says.

Nailed it, I think to myself, or I might have said it out loud.

Ty and now Bryce have gotten me out of my belt and are basically carrying me back to the medical area. They lay me on a stretcher. Ty's putting something on the area that hurts on my head. Trying to stop the bleeding, I guess.

"Hey Mills, focus on me for a second. Okay? Here I am. Over here," Bryce says.

Yes, I see you, Bryce. You're like a foot from my face. Again, I'm not sure if I'm saying that out loud or just thinking it. His face looks blurry.

"Hey. You're okay. We're all okay. We're back in the plane, headed home. Ty's just fixing up a few scratches you have on your head. No big deal. You're fine. Okay?"

I think I'm nodding at him, but to make sure, I eek out, "Okay."

He sits down beside the stretcher, his hand resting on my shoulder. Ty seems to be done doing whatever he was doing. My head hurts, but it doesn't feel like it's leaking anymore. I close my eyes for what feels like a minute, but when I wake up, I realize it's been more than that. Ty and Bryce are gone. Mason has taken their place. He's sitting with his back against my stretcher, sleeping.

I feel more focused now. I try to remember what happened, and it all comes roaring back. The hike down the mountain, Haroun Hadzic, the interrogation, the firefight, the helicopter out, and then blank. I shake my head a little, trying to remember, but it's not there. I suddenly remember what Haroun said to me about Yusef being in Sarajevo, and it comes crashing back to me why I'm on this trip. I need to get to my computer and start a target package for Yusef.

I sit up gently so I won't wake Mason, but he springs up the second I move.

"Whoa, whoa, Mills. Where are you going? Lay back down." He's trying to gently push me back on the stretcher.

"No, I'm fine. I need to work."

"Millie, there's plenty of time to work. You need to be still."

I manage to sit up on the stretcher without him pushing me back down. I notice his hands at the ready in case I get dizzy.

"Mason, I'm fine. I need to get up." I start to get off the table. He grabs my shoulders to steady me, making sure I'm not going to fall over.

"I can stand. I'm good," I insist.

"Come over here with me for a second," he says as his hand makes it to my lower back, pushing me toward a seat away from the medical area.

"Sit down. Let me check you out."

It's not a request, so I sit. He runs me through a battery of tests, mainly testing my eyes and my focus. I pass.

"Okay, let's just sit here for a second. Make sure you're good," he says as he sits down beside me. "Do you remember what happened?"

"Yeah. Mostly. I don't remember getting from the helicopter to the plane."

"Yeah, you fainted when you were getting out of the helo. I carried you in here."

"I fainted? Wow. I'm so sorry."

"Why are you sorry you fainted? It's not your fault. Just kind of happens."

"Have you ever fainted on a mission? Or any of the guys?"

"Mills, we're trained operators. We do this every day. We're used to it. Most people haven't been in a full-out firefight. You did good."

"I didn't do anything."

"You did what you were told, and in that situation, that's all we expect of you."

"I could have gotten you all killed."

"Nothing you did endangered our lives. I asked you to do exactly what we told you to do, and that's what you did. That was perfect."

"I've never even been shot at, much less that," I say more quietly than I intended.

"You did good, Millie. We got the information we went in for, and we all got back safe. It's a good day."

Chapter Twenty-Six

After we land, I see her walking toward her car with her keys in her hand. I follow her.

"You're not driving yourself home." I grab her keys out of her hands before she can react.

"I feel fine now. Just a little headache, but I'm okay to drive." She holds out her hand, expecting me to return the keys. I don't.

"I need to dump my gear, and then I'll take you home." I walk away without looking back, her keys still in my pocket.

Ty walks over to me. "Mase, she probably needs to stay at the hospital tonight. She got dinged pretty good. She'll need to be monitored."

"I'll stay at her place tonight. I'll do the concussion protocol." Ty stops. I know what he's thinking.

"Maybe not the best idea, man." Ty's the quietest person I've ever met, but man, he's an observer. He always knows what's going on.

"It's not a problem." I lock eyes with him. He shrugs. He's not going to question me twice. Never does. None of them do. That's what makes them great operators.

After I dump my stuff in my locker, I go back out to the parking lot to find Millie sitting on her car hood, hugging her knees, her head in her lap.

"Millie, you okay?" I rub her back lightly.

She bolts upright when she feels my hand on her back. Sitting up so quickly makes her dizzy, and she starts swaying.

"Easy, slugger," I say as I steady her and help her down from the car. I put my arm around her shoulders and lead her over to my truck. She doesn't try to shake my arm off. I'm not sure she has the energy.

When we get to her hotel, I lift her down out of the truck and follow her to her door. I still have her keys, so I unlock the door. She walks in, turns around, and looks up at me as she starts closing her door. "Thanks for driving me home, Mason. I appreciate it."

I block the door gently with my hand. "Millie, I'm not leaving. I'm staying here tonight. You might have a concussion. I need to check you a few times during the night to make sure your symptoms don't get worse."

I've already walked in, and closed the door. I look back at her. She's still in the clothes she wore the night before. She's dirty and blood-stained. And, she looks like she hasn't slept in a month.

"Millie, why don't you take a shower, and get some fresh clothes on?"

She looks down at herself, and runs her hand across the

blood stain on her shirt like she's just starting to remember what happened last night.

"You okay?" I'm half expecting her to break down, but she just nods, and heads back to her bedroom. "Yell at me if you need help. I'm going to make us something to eat."

I walk to the kitchen as quickly as possible so I won't be any further tempted to follow her into the shower. Not like this. Not when she's this weak.

I hear the shower starting, and walk into her bedroom to find her clothes on the floor. I pick them up and open the closet to find a dirty clothes bag. Her robe is hanging on the closet door. It's blue with white, fluffy sheep all over it. It's perfectly her, and it makes me smile. Against my better judgment, I decide to take the robe to her. I turn the bathroom handle. Locked. That makes me smile. She knows I knock down doors for a living.

The shower turns off as I enter the bathroom. "Hey, I brought your robe in for you," I say softly. I don't want to scare her.

She peeks around the shower curtain looking at me, confused, but not mad. I know what she's thinking.

"I picked the lock," I say. "The training comes in handy sometimes."

"Well at least you didn't kick it down," she says as she takes the robe. "Wait, this robe is warm. Did you put it in the dryer first?"

I'm suddenly embarrassed. I don't get that way much. "Um, I mean, yeah, I thought you'd like it warm."

She pulls open the shower curtain, now fully wrapped in the white, fluffy sheep robe. "Look at you," she says. "All this alpha male bullshit, and you're actually a cream puff underneath."

"I don't know what a cream puff is, but I'm going to guess I'm definitely not that." I give her my hand to help her step out of the bathtub. She takes it.

I stand there for a second, not letting go of her hand. She looks so soft and vulnerable right now. God, it's killing me. *Snap out of it. Not like this*, I tell myself again. I let go of her hand and walk out of the bathroom. "Are you hungry? I couldn't find much in your refrigerator, but I can make us some pasta or something."

"I'm really tired. Is it okay if I just sleep?" She's made her way over to the bed and is crawling under the sheets. I follow her and help her pull the blankets up around her. She looks up at me, covered up to her chin with blankets, looking so small in the big king-size bed. "Mase, you really don't have to stay here. I'm fine. I feel fine."

"I'm going to stay. I'll wake you up in a few hours to check on you. Okay?"

"Okay," she whispers already half asleep. I sit on the side of the bed, watching her sleep for a few minutes. I don't know what I'm feeling, but I've definitely never felt it before. It's not just lust. I mean it is that. God, I want to be with her. But, it's not just that. I want to hold her, protect her. I want to talk to her, laugh with her. I just want to be near her.

I finally break myself away from her. I fix myself something to eat and watch *SportsCenter*. By the time I'm done, it's been two hours. I need to wake her up and check on her. I brush the mass of wet strawberry-blonde curls away from her face. She's sound asleep. I shake her gently. "Millie," I say softly.

She opens her eyes, sleepy and confused. "Hey," she manages to say as she tries to sit up. I pull her up gently. As I do, the blanket falls down, and I notice the robe has slipped down over her shoulders. I can't stop staring. It's beautiful. She's beautiful, and seeing what I'm seeing, I just want to rip the rest of the robe off and see what else it's hiding. *Not like this*, I repeat over and over in my mind while I quickly adjust her robe back onto her shoulders. She's so out of it, she doesn't even register what happened.

"Hey, Mills, I need to turn on the light to look at your eyes and make sure you're still focusing okay."

"Okay," she says, smiling sweetly. She's slowly starting to remember what's going on.

I take her through a short battery of concussion tests and ask her a few questions. She nails them all. "Good job," I say. "You can go back to sleep."

"Okay," she says looking up at me. "Are you staying here all night? Where are you going to sleep?"

"I'll sleep on the couch."

"I can't even stretch out on that couch fully. There's no way you'll be able to."

"Believe me, I've slept in more uncomfortable places."

"Mason, just sleep in the bed. There's plenty of room. It's not a big deal." She flips over her pillow and snuggles back into the blankets.

I sit there again for a few minutes looking at her, and then take off my shoes, and my shirt, and lay down on the bed. I still have a T-shirt and pants on, and I'm above the blankets. I intend to stay that way. *Not like this, not like this*, I repeat in my head as I fall asleep.

I wake up with a jolt. It takes me a second to remember where I am. I look at my phone. It says I've been asleep for four hours. I find that hard to believe. I never sleep more than an hour or so at a time. I look over. Millie's still sleeping peacefully. I roll over to face her and gently touch her shoulder.

"Millie, you need to wake up again."

She opens her eyes, this time more aware of where she is. "Hey, do we have to do the tests again?"

"Probably not. You seem to know what's going on now. How do you feel?"

"Better. My head doesn't really hurt anymore."

"That's good. Do you feel dizzy or nauseous?"

"I don't think so, just kind of tired still."

"Okay, you sound good. You can go back to sleep. You should be okay until morning, babe." I try to catch myself before it comes out, but it's too late.

Even in the darkness, I can see her eyes widening. "Babe?" she says softly.

"Millie." I scoot a little closer to her, and put my hand on her hip. "Millie, come on, you have to know how I feel about you."

I want to look away from her, but I can't. I have the feeling with that one word, I've just blown the operation I've been working on for weeks.

She puts her hand lightly on my chest. "Mase, we work together. We live in different cities. We have crazy schedules. I have feelings for you, too, but it could never work."

"And, you have a boyfriend," I say turning over on my back, looking at the ceiling. I'm not sure why I brought him up.

"Yeah," she says as if she'd forgotten that part. "Either way, you and I could never work."

"We could figure it out," I say, not really believing it myself. I roll back over to face her. "Millie, I didn't want to talk to you about this tonight. You just need to get some rest. Forget I said anything. We can talk about it later if you want to."

She scoots toward me, and turns until she's spooned into me. I wrap both of my arms around her. We don't say anything else. We just fall asleep like that. I wake up, and it's light out. I look at my phone again. Another five hours. I haven't slept five hours straight since I was a kid. I don't want to let go of her, but I know I need to get back to the base. I'm already late.

I'm hungry again, and I know she hasn't eaten in at least a day, so I text JJ and tell him I'm going to be late. He won't question it. She's still sleeping soundly when I finish making the eggs, so I sit at the kitchen counter to eat my breakfast first before I wake her. As I'm finishing, I hear her coming up behind me quietly. I'm guessing she knows it's impossible to sneak up on me. I turn the stool around. She's standing there in my shirt. Only my shirt. Oh fuck. I think I'm really going to be late.

She maneuvers herself between my legs, and puts her hands on my thighs. I pull her into me, one hand on her back, and the other one buried in her hair. Her lips part just as mine touch down. Her arms climb up my body until they circle around my neck. She's pressed hard against my body, but I keep trying to pull her closer. I want her to be part of me. I want to be inside her. I'm just about to pick her up, and carry her back to bed, when my phone beeps. Fuck you. I ignore it. It beeps again.

She pulls back first. Her cheeks are flush. "You have to see what it is," she says.

She's right. I check. Emergency call from the base. I'm needed there immediately. For the first time since I enlisted, I want to quit. Right here. Right now.

"Go," she says.

"Millie."

"Mason, I know better than anyone what your job is. Go. You're needed. We'll talk later. I'm good. Really, I am."

I leave with her still standing there in my shirt. All I can think about is getting back there. Getting back to her. Getting back to the place we left off.

"Be careful," I hear her say as I close the door.

Chapter Twenty-Seven

VIRGINIA BEACH, VIRGINIA, 2011

"You're not going to wear that out of this house!" Camille was trying her best to keep up with Millie's long strides. "Why can't you dress decently? Everyone knows you're my grand-daughter. They'll talk about us!"

Millie whipped around to face Camille. At sixteen, she had long past reached her breaking point with her grandmother. "It's a T-shirt, Camille. A T-shirt. Settle down."

"A T-shirt with the devil's V right there in front." Camille formed a V with two fingers, waving them accusingly in the air at Millie's barely exposed cleavage.

"Good God, you're losing it." Millie pushed the screen door extra hard so it would make the loudest sound possible when it slammed.

"I'm going to tell your dad about this—taking the Lord's name in vain while you're dressed like that," Camille said to the door.

Millie got in her car and took a deep breath. It's the only

place she felt at peace anymore. Mack had bought her the car for just that reason. He knew she'd have to escape the house regularly just as he had at that age.

She put the car in reverse quickly just in case Camille tried to chase her out of the house. She'd done it before, and she was only getting crazier with age. Beatrice told Millie years ago that Camille had gotten pregnant with Mack when she was a teenager. She said Camille was just trying to prevent Millie from ending up with the same fate. But they both knew Camille was only worried about Camille, and about saving her own reputation.

Most days, Millie didn't know how she'd make it sixty more days until Mack retired. They were planning to move to San Diego right after her graduation. She couldn't wait to finally be free of Camille. *Two more months*, Millie thought as she eased the car onto the highway.

With the summer heat, being on the highway was the only way she could get enough of a breeze through the windows to cool off. The old VW's air conditioner had stopped working years ago, if it had ever worked at all, and the car's black seats made it especially oppressive. But it was a car, and a car meant freedom.

Millie was lost in her thoughts when she saw the sign: "Virginia Beach, Next Four Exits." She spun her head around to make sure she was seeing it right. Somehow, she'd driven an hour without even registering where she was going. She'd never been to visit her dad in Virginia Beach. He always came home when he had free time, even if it was just for a few hours.

Despite her hesitation, Millie took the exit that pointed

toward the naval base. She felt something pulling her closer and closer to the base until she was driving to the guarded entrance.

"Can I help you, ma'am?" An armed guard approached the car.

Mack had trained her on firearms since she was a little kid. She had become an accomplished shooter, but she was still uncomfortable seeing someone wearing a gun. It reminded her that her dad armed and fighting somewhere in the world. It always sent chills down her spine thinking about the what if . . .

"Ma'am? Are you all right?" The guard leaned farther down in her window.

"I'm here to see my dad," she said slowly. "His name is Mack Marsh. He's a SEAL."

Millie didn't even know if this was where he worked when he was home.

"What's your name?" The guard took his eyes off her to look at the clearance list.

"Millie—Millie Marsh—but he doesn't know I'm coming." She started to feel as stupid as she thought she probably sounded.

"Ma'am, we don't allow unscheduled visits from civilians." He stopped suddenly when he saw her big eyes looking up at him. He sighed. "Pull up over by the orange cones. Turn off your car, and wait there."

He shook his head as she smiled at him. *That girl has never been told no in her life by any man,* he thought as he watched her long, blonde hair blow gently as she drove to where he told her to park.

Millie was jolted out of her thoughts when she heard a jeep screech to a halt by the side of her car. She saw Mack jump out and sprint to the driver's side of her car. He yanked open the door.

"Millie! What's wrong? What are you doing here?" When she saw how worried he was, she burst into tears, suddenly ashamed that she had bothered him here.

Mack pulled her to a standing position and hugged her, instinctively looking her over to see if she was injured. "Millie, sweetie, what's wrong? Are you hurt?"

He pulled her back a little bit so he could look at her face, the tears still flowing down.

"I'm an idiot," she said. He could barely understand her through the sobs.

"You're a what? Millie, what is happening?"

"I'm an idiot," she said, her voice shaking. "I had a fight with Camille, and I got in my car to take a drive to clear my head, and all of a sudden I ended up here. I shouldn't have bothered you."

She started crying harder again. "Millie, sweetie, you are never bothering me." Mack kissed her lightly on the top of the head.

"I know you're working. This was a stupid idea," she said.

"I have to go back to work in a bit, but I have like an hour. Are you hungry? We could go get something to eat."

She shook her head no against his chest.

"Okay, then let's go over to the visitors' area," Mack said, rubbing her back gently, "and we can talk a little bit. Okay? C'mon, you can ride in a jeep."

Mack whistled to the guard, pointing at the VW. "Okay, if

she leaves this here for an hour?" He barely waited for the reply. He knew no one ever said no to the SEALs on the base.

"Yeah, all good. I'll keep my eye on it." The guard quickly moved his eyes from Millie to the VW when he saw the way Mack was looking at him.

Mack watched Millie crawl into the jeep. Her cutoffs were barely covering what desperately needed to be covered.

She looked up at him. "What?"

He shook his head and sighed. He drove over to the picnic tables by the visitors' lot. "You thirsty?" he asked as she climbed up to sit on one of the tables. She nodded.

"I'm going to go inside and grab us a few bottles of water. Wait here," he ordered.

"You know, I'd prefer a beer if you have any in there," she said, smiling.

He turned around, continuing to walk backward. "You're not funny, Millie. Not even a little bit."

She smiled as she watched him disappear into the building. She'd felt like a complete idiot a couple minutes before, and now she felt happier than she had in days. He always made her feel that way.

"Ma'am, you lost?" Millie turned around to see a gorgeous man approaching her. He was sweating, like he had just gotten done working out. His T-shirt was tucked into the band of his shorts. Millie's eyes drank in the rippling muscles of his tattoo-covered chest. She didn't seem to have use of her voice at the moment.

He smiled, clearly used to the effect he had on women. "My name's Mason. What's your name?"

She took his extended hand. "Um," she said, trying to

remember what he had asked her, "Millie, and um no, I'm not lost. I'm waiting for my dad."

He smiled and put his foot on the bench next to her. He leaned forward so he was only inches from her. "Oh, is your dad navy? What's his name?"

Millie stared at the trident tattoo on his shoulder, trying desperately to remember her dad's name. "Um, his name is Mack Marsh."

Mason quickly pulled his leg down and backed up two steps. "Mack Marsh is your dad?"

"Yes, Mack Marsh is her dad." Mack had come out of the side door to see one of their new recruits talking to his daughter. He wasn't pleased.

"Mack, I just met your daughter," Mason said a little too loudly as he stumbled farther back away from her.

"You mean my sixteen-year-old daughter?" Mack said, glaring at Mason.

"She's sixteen?" Mason realized he'd made a mistake by looking back at Millie. "Look at the time," he said as he pointed to his bare wrist, walking away quickly.

Millie watched him walk away until Mack grabbed her jaw and pushed it back in his direction.

"Millie," he said, looking directly into her eyes. "He is a SEAL. You will never date a SEAL. Never. Do you understand me?"

"What's wrong with SEALs? You're a SEAL." She tried to steal another glance at Mason as she turned to toss the bottle cap into the trash can.

"Because I'm a SEAL, I know what horrible boyfriends and husbands we make," he said, trying to regain her focus.

"And, besides, you're too young to think about that. Shouldn't you still be playing with dolls?"

"I never played with dolls. You've had weapons in my hands since I was five."

"I stand by that decision." *Especially with the way I just saw that rook staring at you,* he thought.

"Maybe I'll be the first female SEAL," she said. "I mean, isn't that why you taught me all that stuff—the weapons, self-defense? My school counselor said I could write my ticket in the military."

"No, Millie, you're meant for something else. You don't want to spend your life like this. You're a butterfly. You need to be free."

"A combat-ready butterfly," she said.

"Nothing wrong with that. Even butterflies need to know how to kill unwanted suitors."

"I think killing them might be a slight overreaction," she said.

Mack shrugged, not convinced. Millie laid her head on his shoulder and laughed. All she wanted was for the next couple months to speed by, so she could move in with him, and just be his daughter.

"Mack." Millie looked up to see a man in uniform standing behind them.

"Hey, Chase," Mack said. "This is my daughter, Millie."

"Oh, wow. Hey, Millie. The last time I saw you, you were still a baby. How old are you now?"

"Sixteen. Almost seventeen."

"Sixteen. She's sixteen," Mack said.

"Well, it's so nice to finally meet you. Mack talks about you non-stop."

Millie smiled. "Thank you. It's nice to meet you, too."

"Mack, we've got a meeting. I'm sorry to interrupt, but you've got to be in there."

"I know. I'll be there in a minute," Mack said.

"Nice to meet you, Millie," Chase said as he walked back toward the building.

"Nice to meet you, too!"

"Sweetie, I've got to go back to work, but I'll be down there this weekend to pick you up. Okay?" Mack said as he helped Millie into the jeep.

They drove in silence back to her car.

Mack hugged Millie tightly. "Drive safely back home, and text me when you get there."

Millie nodded her head and gave him one last squeeze. "I love you, Daddy. More than anything in the world."

He kissed her on the head. "We'll be together soon, Millie. Only two more months."

Chapter Twenty-Eight

After Mason left this morning, I knew what I had to do. I packed up and left Virginia Beach for good. If I was going to finish what I started, I couldn't have any more distractions, and Mason had become a huge distraction.

My boss agreed to send me back to Bosnia so I could focus on finding Yusef Hadzic. His father had given me a little to go on, so I'll start there and stay in Bosnia for as long as they let me.

I'm set to fly out tomorrow with just enough time to tie up some loose ends, which unfortunately includes the dinner I promised Drew. I'm dreading it, but if it has to happen to finally end our relationship, then it's going to happen before I leave.

Drew's waiting for me outside the restaurant when my car pulls up. Surprisingly, he's smiling. He hugs me and puts his arm around my shoulders. "Hey, you look good. Our table should be ready," he says, guiding me towards the door.

I think for a second about just ending it with him on the street, and getting back into my car and heading home, but he has a firm grip on my shoulders. I let him guide me into the restaurant.

The minute we walk in, I sense Mason in the room. I can feel his eyes on me, hear his breathing, smell his scent. My eyes dart around the room to find him. I don't see him, but I know he's here watching me from some remote corner of the room.

"Are you okay? You look like you saw a ghost," Drew says. He grabs my arm and pulls me after the maître d who leads us to our table.

As we walk through the dining room, I suddenly realize what it must be like to have a rifle leveled at you. That little target light right on your chest, following you everywhere you move. Mason's definitely here, and he's tracking me.

Drew orders the wine. I try to focus on the business at hand, but I'm finding it hard to even have small talk. I excuse myself to use the restroom. I head that way, but make a quick move to the patio door where I'm out of Drew's sight. I get outside, weave through the patio tables, and walk around a wall until I'm completely out of sight of the restaurant. I've barely stopped when I can feel Mason behind me.

"What are you doing here?" I ask without turning around.

"You know what I'm doing here," he growls.

"You can't be here, Mason. I'm with my boyfriend." I don't tell him I'm here to break up with Drew. I want him to think we're still together. I want him to leave.

He puts his hands on my shoulders. I try to shake them off with no luck. He pulls me back toward him while he turns me to face him. He's positioned me about five inches from his body, his hands still holding my shoulders firmly. I don't want to look up. I stare at his chest. He's breathing hard. I watch his chest rise and fall, transfixed by it.

"Why did you leave?" His voice is gruff and edgy.

I try to shake off his hands again, and this time he lets me. I take a step back and look up at him. "I had to get back to D.C. This is where I live."

"You haven't answered any of my calls." He leans back on the wall so we're almost face-to-face. He tries to grab my hand, but I jerk it away from him.

"I've been busy, Mason," I say as I take another step back.

"So, the other night, that morning, it just didn't happen?"

I don't reply.

"Millie, look at me. Just look at me for a second, please."

I steel myself and look up. "Mason, you've got to leave. I'm sorry. It's too complicated. Please, just go."

"I'm not leaving until you talk to me. Until you tell me why." He steps forward quickly, grabs me, and spins me around. His arms and legs both surround me as he presses me against the wall.

"Mason, don't." My voice barely registers the protest as he starts kissing my neck. My arms instinctively start to climb up his chest.

"I'm here with my boyfriend." My voice keeps trying to protest while my body betrays it.

"But where do you want to be?" His lips move to my face. They're gently exploring my forehead, my cheeks, my nose.

My body melts into him, a small moan escaping from my lips just as his lips find them. God, the way he's kissing me.

Hungry. Aggressive. Not asking for permission. It's every cocky thing I hate in a man. Every man except him.

My mind finally re-engages. I try to push his chest away. It doesn't move. I try to work my way out of his hold, but his arms propel me back to the center like a boxer bouncing off the ropes.

I look up, my eyes pleading. "Mason, please let me go."

He lets me go immediately and steps back, his hands up like he's showing he's not going to hurt me. I turn quickly to go back into the restaurant. Drew's standing there, staring at us.

"Drew," I say quickly. "It's not what it looks like."

"Well, it looked like you were making out with Mountain Man Jack over there," he says, gesturing toward Mason. "Is that what was happening, or am I seeing things?"

Mason takes a step toward him. I slam my arm into his chest. "Don't, Mason. Walk away. I'm not even playing with you now. Walk away."

Mason strokes his beard as he thinks, but then shockingly, turns around and walks toward the parking lot without saying anything.

"Who is he?" Drew demands.

"He's a guy I met while I was traveling. It's not what you think."

"Are you having an affair with him? Are you in love with him?"

"No, Drew, I barely know him. I just met him a few weeks ago."

"Well, you're awfully friendly with him for someone you just met," he says.

"Look, Drew, this isn't about him. It's about me and you, and our relationship. I'm sorry, but it's not working for me anymore. It's over. I don't see much of a point of having dinner tonight. I'm sorry."

"Yeah, it's definitely over, Millie. I can't believe you would do this to me after two years, but maybe I didn't really even know who you were," he says, walking away.

Huge understatement. Just the biggest understatement ever.

"I'm really sorry, Drew. I am," I call after him, but he's already gone.

I need to clear my head a bit, so I decide to walk the mile back to my apartment. I don't spend even a second thinking about Drew. My head is full of Mason. As I turn the corner on to my street, I'm not even surprised when I see his truck pulling up behind me.

He rolls down his window. "You think it's a good idea to walk alone in D.C. at night?"

"I'm pretty positive I had a security detail trailing me most of the way." I keep walking to my place. I hear him parking behind me. I increase my pace.

As I get to the stoop, he's already behind me. "Where's your boyfriend?"

"I don't have a boyfriend," I say. "I just broke up with him."

"That was quick."

"I'm very efficient." I walk past him up to my door. He turns on his heels to follow me up the steps.

As I try to unlock the door, he puts his hand over mine to stop me from turning the key. "Millie, if you want me to leave,

I'll drive away right now. I would never force this, force you, but I just want to know why. Please. There's something you're not telling me. It's not the boyfriend, it's not our work schedules. Tell me why you don't want to be with me, and I'll leave."

I want to tell him so badly. Tell him everything that I overheard Chase saying when I was sixteen, everything that Amar Petrovic told me when we were alone, everything that I know I have to do. I've had so many chances, so many times I could have told Mason, but none more perfect than right now. Just tell him. Tell him, and let him help you figure it out. For once, trust someone to have your back. But, I can't. My mind won't let my voice speak. So instead, I reach up and put my hands on his chest, sliding them up around his neck. He kisses me again instantly. I let him. My mind has stopped resisting.

He picks me up, and I wrap my legs around his waist. He turns the keys in the lock and opens the door, still kissing me hungrily. He slams the door and presses my body up against it. My dress is somewhere up around my chest by this time. His fingers have already found their way down my body, under my dress. They don't even pretend to linger. They go straight inside. One finger. Then two.

God, his hands are huge, and warm, and moving inside me. His fingers push hard against my G-spot. Direct hit. The first moan leaves my lips loudly. He knows he has me then. He's in complete control. My body is his.

My mind's spinning when all of sudden, he's inside me. The feeling of him entering me hard, filling me up, makes me straighten up a bit out of surprise. I hadn't even noticed him unzipping. As I straighten up, he pulls me down further on him, pushing even deeper inside of me.

He's pounding my body against the door so loudly that I know my neighbors can hear us. But I have no power to stop this. I don't want to stop this. I let out a series of sounds I've never even heard before and shudder violently, moaning one last time, longer, softer. My body goes limp against him. He pulls me closer and pushes into me hard one last time. I feel his body shudder. He makes a guttural sound as he cums inside of me.

Everything is suddenly quiet around us. He holds me against the door for a minute as we try to catch our breath, then he pulls himself out of me, and gently lifts me to the floor —kissing the top of my head just as my feet hit the floor\.

I'm still leaning against the door in shock, in excruciatingly sensual shock. "What was that?" I manage to say while still trying to catch my breath.

He smiles. "That was 'I couldn't fucking wait a second longer.' God, Millie, I've wanted to do that since the second I saw you walk in the bar that night you hustled us in pool."

"I did not hustle you. I just had a lucky streak."

"Okay," he says, laughing and pulling me towards him. "Maybe tonight's finally my night to have a lucky streak."

He pulls what's left of my dress over my head and gently kisses me, as he picks me up, and carries me back to the bedroom.

Chapter Twenty-Nine

MASON, WASHINGTON, D.C., 2019

I wake up with my body so tightly wrapped around her that I'm surprised she's still breathing. I had that dream again where someone's trying to take her from me—trying to pull her out of my arms. I can tell that I tightened my grip on her while I was sleeping. We're in the most aggressive spooning position possible.

I lean over her head carefully and see her hair rising and falling with her breath, so I know I haven't squeezed her to death. This is actually comforting to me because that dream is too fucking real. I don't know who the people are trying to take her, but they're not going to win.

I'm getting upset again just thinking about it, so before I start trying to boa constrict her to my body again, I get up to make some coffee. When I get back with two mugs, she's sitting up on the side of the bed, completely naked, with her sexy-ass back turned toward me. My mind jumps back to last night when I was running my hands over her back while I was inside her. It makes me hungry again. She sees me looking and quickly wraps the blanket around herself.

"You know, Mills, I saw all of your body last night. Alllll of it. All night. You don't have to hide it from me now," I say, smiling.

She turns her head slightly to look at me with her back still facing me. I'm buck-ass naked, standing in the doorway with two cups of coffee.

"I know what you saw, Mason. But it doesn't mean you get to see it again." She smiles a little shyly. She definitely wasn't shy last night, but it's so fucking adorable this morning.

"Yeah, it probably does. I think your body kind of likes me." I put the coffee down on the table and crawl in the bed behind her. I start tugging at the blanket that's covering her—hand over hand, reeling her to me. She finally relents and lets the blanket fall, crawling up on my chest.

"Much better," I whisper in her ear as I stroke her hair.

There's something about running my fingers through her hair that turns me on. I'm getting hard again. I take her hand off my chest, and move it down my body. She takes over halfway down, and keeps moving her hand until she's holding me. She gets on top of me and starts licking my chest. She keeps pushing herself down my body, licking and kissing. She's at my stomach when I grab her head and tilt it up so I can see her eyes.

"Babe, you don't have to do that," I growl softly. I want her to go down on me so badly, but I know not all women like to do that, and I don't want her to do anything she doesn't want to do.

She smiles a little devilishly at me, and keeps moving her head downward. "I know I don't have to do it, Mason. But I want to. That's why I'm offering."

Using my own words against me. It's so fucking sexy.

"Fuck," I groan as she takes me in her mouth. I literally could cum in a second, but I hold on. Her hands start playing with my balls as she's licks and kisses her way up and down.

I've finally had enough. I'm about to explode. I reach under her arms and pull her up swiftly, flipping her so I'm on top of her. I slide myself inside her quickly, pumping myself in and out until she starts groaning, and then I let out a loud moan that I'm sure woke up half of the neighborhood.

"Fuuuuuuck, Millie. Fuck. What are you doing to me?" I'm breathing so hard that I think I might need oxygen. Damn, no one has ever been able to manipulate my body like this. I'm always in control, but with her . . . I don't know what's happening.

"Did I hurt you? Are you going to be okay?" She's smiling that sweet, mischievous way that makes her eyes sparkle.

"I think I'm going to make it, but I'm definitely going to need to stop for a reload."

"Babe, seriously, I surrender," she says, collapsing on top of my chest again.

That's the first time she's called me that. "Babe, huh?"

"Does that bother you?"

I lift her head, so I can look her directly in the eyes. "Not at all."

Honestly, it sounds magical coming out of her mouth.

"Millie, I have to go back this morning. I really shouldn't be this far from base at all."

"I know," she whispers as she snuggles a little closer to my chest.

"I don't want to leave."

"I know. I don't want you to leave, but I know."

"Can I take you out again?"

"Did you take me out the first time?" She looks up, laughing.

"Yeah, I guess last night wasn't really a date. I want to make it up to you. Take you some place nice where I can spoil you."

"You know I'm going to be in D.C. for a while now. You're three hours away on a good day. I'm not sure how we're going to keep this going."

"We can make it work. If you want to, we can make it work. Millie, I've never felt this way about anyone. I need to at least try to make it work."

"Mason, you're being deployed in a week. I have no idea where they're going to send me. This would be tough. Right now, it would be really tough. I don't even know when I'm going to see you again."

"Maybe I can get Culver to ask for you to be assigned to us permanently," I say, knowing it's a bad idea, but I'm desperate.

"Mason, c'mon, that wouldn't work any better. You can't be fucking someone you work with."

"You think that's all this was? Me fucking you? Is that what it was for you? Because it's a lot more for me," I say, suddenly feeling very defensive.

"That's not what I meant. It's just bad timing. We both have so much going on right now. You can't quit and move to

D.C. I can't quit and move to Virginia. It's just what it is."
She's being way too practical and realistic, and I'm not liking
it at all. I'm pissed now. I've never been the one in the relationship who cares too much. It's starting to feel like
that now.

"Seriously, Millie. It was just sex for you. Damn, I totally
misread this situation."

"Mason, no, it's not, it wasn't just sex. It's just," she says,
hesitating.

"It's just what? What aren't you telling me? And it's not
your boyfriend or your job or your travel schedule or that it
would be a long-distance relationship. What is it? You're
keeping something from me. Damn it, Millie, what is it?"

She sits up. "Mason, I'm leaving for Bosnia later tonight.
Can we talk about this when I get back?"

"Wait, what? You're going back to Bosnia? Why? Did you
find Hadzic?"

"No, I haven't found him yet, but the agency has agreed to
let me work out of the embassy while I'm searching for him. I
don't know how long I'm going to be over there."

"Why aren't we going over with you? Have you talked to
Culver about this?"

"Not yet. There's no reason for you guys to be over there
with me. I don't even know if the intel Hadzic's father gave
me is real yet. I need to be over there, so I can monitor the
situation in person."

"And if you find him, what happens then if we're not with
you?"

"Well, it depends on when and if I find him. Your team's
going to be deployed in Afghanistan for months, so it might

not be your team that gets called in. There's a team in Germany now that will be closer."

"Hell no," I say. "We're the ones that got you this far. We're going to be the ones that finish this with you."

"Well, that's really not my call. And, I have to find him first. This might be a moot point. I'm not even sure if he's in Bosnia. It might be months—years—before I find him."

"So, you're just going to hang out in Sarajevo for years?"

"Of course not, but I'm going to be over there for as long as they'll let me."

"What is it about this guy? Why are you so invested in him?"

"I've been chasing him since I got to the agency. This is the first real lead I've had on him. It's the first lead the agency has had in years."

"There's still something you're not telling me."

"Mason, I leave in six hours. I have a ton to do before I leave. I'm sorry I didn't tell you about this earlier, but it just happened within the last day," she says. "With Drew, and everything with him, and trying to get everything together, I've been distracted. You know how it gets before you leave on deployment. It's a lot."

My phone's been blowing up for the last fifteen minutes. I haven't looked at it. I'm not sure what to say to Millie right now, so I roll over and pick it up. Emergency text from the base, and I'm three hours away at best.

"I've got to go, Millie," I say as I get out of bed and search for my clothes. "I don't know what to say about all of this, but maybe it's better if I just leave. You're right about our jobs. Maybe it would be too complicated."

She sits on the bed looking up at me; her eyes are sad, but she doesn't say anything. I kiss her on the head as I walk out.

"I'll call you later," I say as I'm shutting the door.

When I get in the car, I call Culver, and explain where I am. He's pissed, but keeps it under control. I tell him about Millie going over to Bosnia by herself, and he gets really pissed. He tells me he's going to take care of that, and that he'll cover for me until I get back to the base.

As I drive out of D.C., my gut's telling me I've seen Millie for the last time. Like my dream where the guys are trying to pull her out of my arms, I feel like she's being ripped away from me, and for the first time in my life, I feel totally helpless.

———————

Chapter Thirty

This was the first time Millie had been to Camille's house since Mack died. It had taken her almost two months to get enough strength to come back to collect the rest of her belongings. As she pulled into the driveway, the memories came flooding back.

She'd been sitting on the front porch waiting for Mack to pick her up. He had a week's vacation. They were going to fly to San Diego to look for houses, and to register her for school.

She'd seen the strange car driving up and then Mack's friend, Chase, who she'd just met at the base the week before, getting out of the car. She thought for a second that he'd driven Mack to the house. Then she saw how he was dressed —the dark, formal uniform. She remembers looking up at him as he approached her. His clean-shaven face was absolutely void of expression.

She only had vague memories of the rest of that day. She remembered Chase picking her crumpled body off the porch and holding her as she sobbed. She remembered him leaving her sitting on the lawn chair as he went inside to tell Camille that Mack had died. She remembered hearing yelling, and then she remembered Chase helping her pack a bag, and loading her limp body into his car. Millie had stayed with Chase's family since that day. She'd never asked him why he brought her there or what Camille had said to him. She hadn't really had the energy to think about it until now.

Chase told Millie that Mack had wanted to be cremated, and his ashes distributed at sea. She had gone out on the boat with his team members. She released his ashes when they told her it was time. They were all talking to her, hugging her, holding her, but she didn't remember anything they said. Camille hadn't been at the funeral. Millie didn't know if anyone had invited her. She hadn't even thought about it.

After the funeral, Millie didn't leave her bed for weeks. Chase's wife, Mariel, took care of her. She finally got Millie to get out of bed for a walk one day. And since then, Millie had been living with them like she was one of their kids. She hadn't even realized she'd been living there for months until she overheard them talking last night.

"Chase, she can't live here forever. She's not our child," Mariel said.

"Keep your voice down. It's only been a couple months, Mar. She's still working her way through it."

Millie went down to them when she heard them talking. Mack always taught her to confront her problems head on.

"Hey," she said as she entered the kitchen. "I'm so sorry I've been here this long. I'll move out tomorrow."

"Oh my God, Millie, you weren't supposed to hear that."

Mariel ran over to Millie and hugged her. "You can stay here as long as you want. I'm sorry."

"No, you're right. You've got enough going on. You've been so nice to me, but it's time I figure out what I'm going to do next."

Chase came over and hugged both of them. "Millie, you can stay here forever if you want. We'll help you figure out what your next step is going to be. Okay?"

Millie nodded. "I don't want to go back to the Outer Banks. I've decided I want to drop out of high school and get my GED. And then I've been thinking about starting college early. Dad left me some money. That's probably what I want to spend it on."

"Well, you're going to stay here until all that's done and then as long as you want after that," Chase said. "And, you're welcome back here every summer, every holiday forever."

Millie sat in her car, staring at Camille's house, for a good thirty minutes before she got up the courage to walk in. The front door was unlocked, as usual, but the house was eerily quiet. Camille almost always had something going on in the kitchen. Millie checked there. It was quiet, clean, nothing on the stove. Millie thought maybe Camille had gone out. But, she never went out. She never went anywhere. Millie looked at the clock on the microwave—two o'clock. Camille would never be outside in the middle of the day. She hated the sun and heat. Millie always wondered why she lived in a beach town. She hadn't once seen Camille step foot in the sand.

Millie decided to just go upstairs to her room and start packing. She figured Camille would show up sooner or later. She stopped to glance in Camille's room on the way to her own, although she knew Camille wouldn't be in there. Camille believed a bedroom was only to be used during sleeping hours. She yelled at Millie many times for being in her bedroom at all hours of the day. Millie peeked in, and saw Camille lying on her bed. She knew at once that Camille was dead. She would never take a nap. Never.

Millie stood in the doorway for a second, filled with a weird mix of shock, sadness, and relief. She walked over to get a closer look at her. Camille looked beautiful. She was wearing her best dress, and had full hair and makeup done. Millie would have never expected anything less.

She looked over at the side table, and saw two envelopes sitting next to an empty bottle of sleeping pills. One said "My Will" in Camille's writing, and the other said, "Millie" in her dad's writing. She picked up the one that said "Millie," and ran her hand over her name. Just seeing his handwriting brought the tears back to her eyes.

She shook her head a few times to clear the fog, put the "Millie" envelope in her bag, and went downstairs to call the sheriff. She sat on the front porch while they did their thing. She heard the coroner say to the sheriff that Camille had been dead for less than a day. Millie knew that somehow Camille had telepathically ordered her to come to the house today. The whole city would have talked if they'd found her looking anything but fresh.

Millie saw the funeral home carrying Camille's body out of the house. She realized she was sitting on the same lawn chair she'd been on when she heard her dad died. This time, she was sitting straight up, no tears. The only thing she felt was tired.

"Millie." The sheriff stood over her.

Millie looked up at him. He handed her the "My Will" envelope. "I found this by the bed."

"Yeah, I saw it. I'm not sure if I should have it. Does she have an attorney or something?" She realized how stupid she sounded asking him that about her own grandmother.

He didn't seemed fazed. "I think old Dooley downtown is the one who handles her business if you want to take it to him. Sorry for your loss."

He walked to his car and left. The hearse with her body was already gone. Millie didn't know what to do. She sat on the porch and finally decided to do what she'd come there to do. She went upstairs, packed up her stuff, and left.

She drove back to Chase and Mariel's house after she dropped the will off at the Dooley Law Office. Mariel almost had a heart attack when Millie told her Camille was dead. Mariel started crying, telling Millie she could stay with them for the rest of her life. Millie ended up comforting Mariel all night.

The next morning, Mr. Dooley called Millie to tell her that Camille had left everything to her—the house and two acres of beach-adjacent property. Millie was shocked. She hadn't really thought about who Camille would leave her things to after Mack died, but she was certain it wasn't going to be her. Dooley said there was a note from Camille to Millie attached to the will. He texted her a picture of it.

· · ·

Millicent -

Your dad gave me a letter when you were a baby to give to you in case he didn't come home from one of his missions. Well, he didn't come home from one. I didn't give it to you then, and I probably should have thrown it away.

He asked me not to read it. I didn't. It's probably full of the nonsense you two were always talking. I never understood why he coddled you so much. I've told you from day one, you have to be tough. It's the only way you will survive.

You've never listened to one piece of advice I've given to you, but I hope you listen to this one. Throw his letter away. Don't read it. Move on with your life. I've left you everything. You'll have plenty of money to get away from this town, and start a new life without him, and without me.

For once, have some sense in your head. Move on.
Camille

Millie laughed for the first time since Mack died. She didn't know what she had expected Camille's last words to her to be, but she thought those were pretty close. She still had Mack's letter in her purse. She took it out and stared at it for a few minutes before she opened it. She wasn't sure she was ready to read it, but she knew she had to.

December 12, 1995

.   .   .

Millie,

If you're reading this, I'm probably dead. I don't know how it happened, but I guess it was my time. I'm so sorry to leave you alone in this life, but just know, every day, that I loved you more than anything in the world. Becoming your dad transformed me into the person I was meant to be. You saved me, Millie, and please know all of the decisions I made along the way were to save you. If you ever need me, just look up in the sky, I'll be there waiting for you.

With all my love,

Dad

Millie curled up in a ball on her bed and cried for a good hour before she heard Chase and Mariel talking downstairs. She dragged herself out of the bed and went downstairs to tell them about the letter. As she got to the bottom of the stairs, she heard her name.

"Chase, I've been married to you for twenty years. I know how the SEAL family works. When someone dies, we all fill in the void, but we can't be Millie's parents. She's almost seventeen. She has to find her own life."

"Mar, it's about more than loyalty. There's something I haven't told you." Chase hesitated. "Actually, a lot I haven't told you."

"What haven't you told me?" Mariel's voice raised a few octaves.

"It's who Millie is, who her mother is . . ." Chase's voice trailed off.

"You told me her mother died in an accident right after Millie was born. She was from New York, right?"

"No, she wasn't, and that's not now she died. Look, I can't tell you everything, but Millie's mom was a woman we worked with in Bosnia named Nejra. She was killed right after Millie was born."

"Killed? Like murdered?"

"She was from a strict Muslim family. She was single, pregnant. No one knew who the father was. Her brother apparently killed her in what they call an honor killing after she had the baby—to bring back honor to his family."

"What are you talking about? That's crazy. And, Mack knew about all of this?"

"Yeah, he only knew after it all happened. He didn't even know Nejra was pregnant. They had a fling when we were in Bosnia. Nothing serious. We were long gone from Bosnia by the time he found out. He got a phone call like six months after we got back. It was a man. He didn't know who, maybe Nejra's brother. He told Mack that Nejra had his baby, and had been killed for it. He told him where the baby was. Mack told me about the call. I thought it was some kind of set-up. He wanted leave to go over and find the baby. I told him not to go. I begged him not to go, but he was going to go whether I gave him the time or not, so I told him he could take his two weeks personal time. A week and a half later, he shows up back in the States with the baby, with Millie."

"Jesus, Chase, did he kidnap her?"

"Well, I mean technically, she's his daughter. He had her tested when he got back but yeah, he just took her."

"How long have you know about this?"

"From day one, he told me everything."

"This is crazy, Chase. Mack kidnapped a child from a foreign country. He could have gone to jail. You could have gone to jail for hiding his secret. What the fuck were you thinking? Her family in Bosnia has probably been looking for her all these years."

"The only family she has is her uncle, and that's the part of the story I can't tell you—who her uncle is. But, let's just say, Mack was right to get Millie away from him. He likely would have killed her."

"Who's her uncle? Is he dangerous? Did he kill Mack?"

"I can't talk about that, Mar, but the reason Mack and I stayed silent all these years was to protect Millie, and that's why Millie has to stay close to us now that Mack's gone. I told Mack I would never let anything happen to her if he died, and I won't."

"Chase, we have two children of our own. If having Millie here puts them in danger, we can't keep her here. I won't do it."

"I don't think Millie's uncle has any idea where she is. Honestly, he might not even be alive anymore."

Millie walked back upstairs quietly, Mack's letter still in her hand. She shoved the letter back into her purse and sat down on the bed. She couldn't believe what she just heard. She couldn't believe her dad had lied to her all those years.

"All of the decisions I made along the way were to save you."

She knew Chase wouldn't tell her anymore if she asked him, so she decided not to tell him she had overheard the conversation. For the first time since Mack died, Millie felt like she had a reason to live. She had to find out who her mother was, and if her uncle had killed her mom and maybe even her dad. And if her uncle was still alive, Millie knew she had to find a way to kill him.

Chapter Thirty-One

MILLIE, SARAJEVO, BOSNIA, 2019

After being in Sarajevo for only a week, we had a positive sighting of Yusef Hadzic. Our agent—who had been sitting on his sister's house—saw him leaving there around midnight two nights ago. Unfortunately, our agent wasn't able to get to the street fast enough to tail him, but he did get good photographs of him. We identified him at a one hundred percent match to be Hadzic.

I spent the better part of the morning on the phone with my boss. The higher-ups in D.C. are going nuts. They can't believe that we found, and then lost, Hadzic. I haven't slept at all since we located him. I'm trying to put the pieces together of where he went after he left the sister's house. I've already been to her house to interview her, her husband, and her kids. I believe what they told me—that they don't know where he goes when he leaves their house. He could even be back in Afghanistan by this time.

My eyes are blurry from looking at satellite images. I need

some fresh air. I decide to go for a jog. I haven't talked to Mason since he left my house that morning, but I can hear his voice in my head warning me not to jog alone. I do it anyway. I need to clear my head, and I don't need anyone distracting me.

The guards barely look at me as I leave the embassy's back gate. I head down a side street and veer off toward the river. As I start to tire out, I realize I've probably gotten a little too far out of the city. I'm almost in the foothills of the mountains. I'm not sure I have the energy to get all the way back to the embassy.

I try to call back to the embassy to get a car to pick me up, but I'm not getting a signal, so I decide to start walking back. My feet hurt and I have a headache. I'm beginning to regret my decision to jog alone. I need some motivation, so I crank up Clapton in my earbuds. Another thing Mason told me not to do. I can hear him in my head. *"Turn down the music, Mills. Be aware of your surroundings."*

I miss him. It's been hard to focus on anything with him occupying a good portion of my brain. As I'm thinking about how much I'd like to see his face right now, I feel someone grab me from behind. My head's so full of thoughts of Mason that for a split second, I think it's him. That thought leaves my head completely when I see the gun in my assailant's hand.

I'm already a step behind, but I react as quickly as my brain lets me. I jab an elbow into the body behind me, and then step down hard on his foot. As the body recoils from me, I turn around to see Yusef Hadzic bent over in front of me. Clapton's still blasting in my ears, making it hard to think. I'm miles out of town. There's nowhere to run, no one to hear me yell.

Yusef begins to straighten up. My only choice is to fight. I kick him in the face before he straightens up the entire way, causing him to fall back a little farther. I follow him, and try to land a good hard kick to his balls, but he's recovered enough to grab my foot. I try to shake loose, but he has a good grip and pulls me closer, raising his gun back up and pointing it at my head.

"Let's stop this nonsense," he says in Bosnian as he clicks the safety off the gun.

I'm sure he's about to shoot me. My dad's face flashes before my eyes. He's smiling at me, and all I can think is that I'm probably going to see him soon.

Another man gets out of the car behind us. "Yusef, enough! Get her in the car now." He's speaking in Pashto. I've never seen this man before.

Yusef throws my foot down and roughly grabs my arm, pushing me toward the car. I start to struggle wildly. I want them to kill me here. I'm not getting in the car. The other man comes up behind me and puts a hood over my head. I start fighting even harder. Just shoot me now, and leave my dead body by the road. One of them picks me up and shoves me into the car as I kick and scream.

"Shut up, you whore." I recognize Yusef's voice. He slaps my hooded face hard enough to make me fall back against the car door.

The other man, who I think is in the driver's seat, yells in Pashto, "Yusef! If you hurt her, he will kill you. Don't touch her again."

I press myself against the car door, hoping it will open and I will fall out of the moving car. I don't know what's ahead of me, so I'd prefer just to die now. The door doesn't move, but I stay pressed up against it. No one is talking. The car's moving fast, and it feels like we're starting to climb a steep road. I'm sure we're headed up into the mountains.

We drive for about an hour before we stop. I try to memorize any sounds I hear. I've managed to turn off my cell phone that's in a hidden pocket in my jogging pants. Hopefully, the battery will stay strong long enough for someone to track my whereabouts. Honestly, I'm not even sure anyone knows that I've left the embassy except the guards, and they barely looked at me.

Someone opens my door from the outside and grabs me before I fall out. I think it's the other man, not Yusef. His hands feel bigger and less aggressive. He starts to lead me down what feels like a dirt path under my feet. I hear some other male voices getting louder as we continue forward. One of them says in Pashto, "Did anyone see you take her?"

Yusef replies no.

The other man who has ahold of my arm says, "Step up."

I climb up four steps and cross a door threshold. I can tell I'm inside now—the wind has stopped hitting me. The man drops my arm, and pulls off my hood. I'm standing in the middle of a foyer of a mountain cabin. There are steps to my left, and I notice someone walking down them. I turn to see an old man.

"Yasmine," he says, looking directly at me.

I don't recognize him. He has a full head of gray hair and a shaggy gray beard. His skin is so wrinkled and worn. It looks like he's been standing on the sun's surface for a week straight.

"You don't recognize me. But why would you?" He's speaking in English with a heavy Bosnian accent. "We haven't seen each other for twenty-five years."

He gets within a foot of me, and I know I have never seen this face. I'm searching for any clues, but nothing's coming to me.

Yusef comes up behind me and slaps me on the back of the head. "You don't remember your uncle?"

The man glares at Yusef. "I apologize for Yusef. You're bringing back bad memories for him. Do you know that he was supposed to marry your mother—my sister—before your father raped her?"

It comes to me like a bolt of lightning striking me on the head. This man is Sayid Custovic. My uncle. I stare at him for a good minute without talking. No one has seen him in decades, and I know now that even if they did, no one would recognize him. He has aged at least fifty years from the last picture I've seen of him.

"Ah, now I can see in your eyes that you know who I am. I'm afraid the cancer in my body has aged me well beyond my years. You, however, look exactly like your mother did the last time I saw her—young and beautiful. She was about your age when she was murdered."

I finally find my voice. "When you murdered her."

"Me? You think I killed my sister? She was the only good thing in my life after our parents—your grandparents— were killed in the war. I wouldn't have hurt a hair on her head."

"Everyone believes you killed her because she was pregnant. An honor killing," I say, glaring at him.

"Yes, that was widely reported. I was supposed to do that. When the elders found out about you, they told me to kill you and your mother. I probably would have killed you eventually if your father hadn't taken you from me. I'm assuming it was him that took you. I never knew for sure. I thought about tracking him for a while, but really he did me a favor by taking you. Your mother would have haunted me forever if I would have killed you."

"If you didn't kill her, who did?"

"When I got back to the house, and found her dead, everyone told me that her heart had just stopped beating, a reaction to delivering you. She looked so peaceful laying there. No gun wounds, no sign of a struggle. I believed them for years. But then Amar told me what really happened. You met Amar, I believe. He's probably the one who told you where to find Yusef's dad. He didn't tell me. You must have had some kind of effect on him, but then, you look just like my sister, and Amar was always in love with her. No bother though. You led me right to Haroun. The fighters that you encountered in those hills around his house were my fighters. They found him right after you got away. You should have stayed. I was living only about ten miles from there at the time. We could have met much earlier."

Out of the corner of my eye, I see Yusef start to shift nervously. The man who drove the car grabs him by the shoulders and forces him to stand still. I glance over to him.

Sayid continues. "Yes, you see Yusef is getting nervous. He hasn't realized until now that I know. I've kept him alive this long because Amar told me you were tracking him. His father told me that he told you where to find Yusef. He never loved Yusef nearly as much as Yusef loved him. He thought he was weak. He always loved me. I think he wished I was his son. And, after all these years, well, what I've done with my life, he admired me even more. I think he hated Americans more than he hated the Serbs and, as you know, I've been able to kill so many Americans in the past few decades. Your father really inspired it all. After what he did to my sister. After he raped her."

"My dad didn't rape her. From what I hear, she was a very strong woman who made her own decisions."

"She was headstrong, and I have no doubt that she wanted to be with your father in that way, but in my mind, it is the man who is at fault for having relations with an unmarried woman. It is rape whether she wants it or not. Yusef's father did not see it that way though. He blamed my sister. Isn't that right, Yusef?"

Sayid looks over at Yusef, who's still being held firmly by the other man. Sayid walks slowly over to him. Yusef starts to stay something, but Sayid holds up his hand, silencing him immediately.

"Amar told me that your father suffocated Nejra, Yusef. And, you moved him into the mountains to hide him from me. All these years you've lied to me, and told me that your father died of a heart attack. He didn't. He died when I put a bullet through his head," Sayid says.

"Sayid, Amar is crazy. You know that he lost his way when he moved his family to Spain. He always resented me because I was to marry Nejra. You know this. He was lying to you about my father," Yusef says.

"But yet, you are the one who hid your father in the mountains, so you could still visit him, but make sure he was out of my sight. I didn't even know that he had killed Nejra until a few months ago. Why did you think you had to hide him from me all these years?" Sayid says.

Yusef stares blankly at him and starts to visibly shake.

"Well, it doesn't matter now. Your father confessed to me before I killed him, so I know now how she died. Finally, I know for sure. You know how unsettled it has made me all these years, and yet you have let me suffer."

"Sayid." Yusef's voice is so quiet that I can barely hear him.

"No, it is much too late for any explanation. You have been a loyal soldier to me for years, but you know how much I have agonized over the years because of her death. And, you chose to let me suffer. It's time for us to say goodbye, my friend."

Sayid turns and walks away from Yusef. He gently takes my arm and starts leading me up the stairs. "My niece, will you help your uncle back up to his room?"

Since there are four armed men following us, I don't feel like I have much of a choice. I take his outstretched arm, and steady him as he walks slowly up the stairs. When we're about half-way up, I hear a gunshot and whip my head around to see Yusef falling to the floor, his head spurting blood everywhere.

Chapter Thirty-Two

I got back to the base from Millie's place in under three hours. I walk into the briefing room. All eyes turn to me, but no one dares say anything. The tension in the room is about to explode. Culver is just telling them that our deployment has been moved up, and we are wheels up to Afghanistan in three hours. He releases the team. They all look at me as they walk out.

"Everything okay, man?" JJ asks as he follows the others out to get his gear. I nod and walk over to Culver.

"We can't just go to Afghanistan. We need to go to Bosnia first. She's going to be over there alone," I say, knowing it's not going to happen.

Culver asks the two analysts who are still in the room to leave. He hasn't taken his eyes off me since I walked in the door. I can't tell if he's about to hit me or fire me, or maybe even both.

"We're not going to Bosnia. I've got that covered. Your

assignment is in Afghanistan, and that's where you're going," Culver says with a steely tone I haven't heard before. At least I haven't heard it directed at me.

"Look, I know you're pissed—"

"Mason, I'm on another-level pissed off at you right now. I thought seriously about taking you off this deployment, and putting your ass on probation. I can't believe the carelessness you've shown in the last day. What if we had an emergency? What if we were wheels up immediately? And, you're fucking three hours away. You have broken so many rules that I don't even know where to start. Get your ass to the ready room, and get on that fucking plane. I don't want to hear anything more from you today. Raine can brief you separately on why our go-date has been moved up to today. I'll tell her you're back."

He spins on his heels and walks briskly out of the room. I'm alone in the room now. My usually well-ordered brain is all over the place. I hear the door open and turn around to see Raine. She's staring at me like she doesn't know if it's safe to come in or not. I try to get control of my thoughts.

"What do you have for me?" I ask, looking at her like everything's normal. She takes a deep breath and dives into the briefing on a few HVTs that have been identified in Afghanistan. They want us over there early to get up to speed before our other team leaves the area. I force myself to concentrate. I need to get my mind back in the game. This is my job, and other lives depend on me being at a hundred percent.

We're about an hour into the flight. I can't sleep as usual. I grab the book I've been trying to read for about a year out of my backpack. I notice something sticking out of it. I open it to find an envelope with my name on it. It looks like a woman's writing. There's a letter inside. I scroll down to the signature. It's from Millie. She must have put it in my backpack before she left for D.C. I'm not sure I even want to read it, but I know I'm not going to be able to concentrate until I do.

Mason -

I haven't told you everything. But you already know that. I wanted to tell you. I almost did so many times. I didn't know any of this until I was seventeen. I overheard my dad's best friend telling his wife about who I really am, and Amar Petrovic finally confirmed it for me that night in Sarajevo when you found me alone in the room with him. I still don't know everything and that's the main reason I haven't told you. Or anyone. I have to find out the truth, and I have to do it on my own. I know you would have tried to stop me.

I think my mother was a woman my dad met when he was working in Bosnia. I'm almost sure of it now. But, I need to hear it from the only person who can tell me for sure. I've been looking for him for eight years, and I can't rest until I find him. I'm sure you've figured out who it is by now, but I can't tell you until I know for sure.

Since my dad died, I didn't think anyone could take care of me the way he did. I was wrong. You can. You have. But, I can't let you in on this one. I'm so sorry, Mason, but I started this alone. I have to finish it alone.

Millie

. . .

I'm sure it must be a joke. The entire letter. It must be some bizarre joke that I'm not understanding right now. I read it a few more times. Is she talking about Sayid Custovic? Is that who she thinks can clear up the mystery for her? I grab the satellite phone and try to call her. It goes right to voicemail. Her phone must be turned off. I try again, and it just rings. This doesn't make any sense. She never turns off her phone.

I bound up the stairs to the plane's upper deck, where the analysts are working. "Clark, track Millie's cell phone," I demand.

"Track her cell phone? What? Are you stalking her now? Don't think I don't see the way you look at her." Her smile quickly goes away when she turns around and sees my face.

"Charlotte, track her cell phone. Now."

She jumps over to her computer, her fingers flying over the keyboard.

"Well, that doesn't make sense." She's making a circle on the screen with her finger. I walk up behind her to see what she's seeing. Her finger's circling a mountain pass just southeast of Sarajevo.

"Culver said she was going to Sarajevo, but why would her phone be up here? And it looks like it's moving. Let me see if I can get a clearer image. Maybe she's just taking a drive in the mountains," she says as I'm already bounding down the stairs to find Culver.

Culver sees me coming at him full speed.

"Millie's gone after Custovic. I had Clark track her cell phone, and it's pinging up in the mountains around Sarajevo. Something's off."

"I told you I had that covered, Mason," he says, now

sounding a little unsure. "You said her phone is pinging in the mountains?"

"Yeah, man, I know you're pissed at me for being with her, but I can feel it. I can feel something's off. We've got to do something."

"Follow me," he says as he grabs the satellite phone. He dials a number.

"Yeah?" A man's voice answers the phone on the other end.

"You have Millie in your sights?" Culver asks with an edgy tone to his voice.

"She's still in the embassy. I haven't see her leave."

"Her cell phone is pinging up in the mountains." Culver heads back up to Clark. I follow.

"What? What the fuck? She hasn't left since she got here. I've been checking all the cars in and out. Nothing."

I don't know who the other guy on the phone is, but I want to punch him so badly right now.

"Leave right now. Head towards the mountains southeast of town. I'm texting you the location. Clark, text Millie's location to this number. Now," Culver hisses.

"You should see this, Captain." Raine has joined us. She points to her screen. "This is where Millie's cell phone stopped."

We both look over to her screen. It's showing a house with about twenty armed men in the yard.

"A car just pulled up, and two men pulled a hooded person out of the car." Raine flips over to another screen to show the image she captured. "It looks like a woman. And, I isolated the men. That one there, that's Yusef Hadzic. One hundred percent certainty."

Culver's face is about to explode. "Mason, Red Team is already inbound from Germany. Get on the phone with them. Find out where they are, their ETA, and let them know what they're facing. And, tell them there's a local asset already on the ground there. He'll meet their helo."

"Roger that." I'm fully focused now. If I'm not going to be able to get there myself, my brothers are going to have me covered. I need to help them do their jobs now.

———————

Chapter Thirty-Three

MILLIE, TREBEVIĆ MOUNTAINS, BOSNIA, 2019

We get to Sayid's bedroom and go inside. He tells the armed men to wait outside. He motions for me to take a seat over by the window. He sits opposite of me. There's a gun on the table between us that's closer to him. I know I could beat him to it, but there's no way I'd get past all the other guns in the house, so I just sit down for now.

"I wanted to tell you a little bit about your mother. Would you like that?" He's smiling at me like we're just chilling out at a family reunion. I don't say anything. He continues anyway.

"Her name was Nejra. You look just like her. You definitely have her eyes. Has anyone ever told you that? I'm guessing your hair is from your dad. I never knew who he was until I found out you were searching for me. Amar told me. Don't let that disappoint you. I'm guessing you had some kind of connection with him. Your mother did. Nejra and Amar were best friends. He called your father to tell him about you.

He confessed everything to me when I found him in Portugal where you tried to hide him from me. He didn't have much of a choice. I would have killed his family. I could tell by the way he spoke of you that he cared about you, but he cares about his own family more. He told me your name, and I looked up your father. He was killed by Al-Qaeda which was good. I wish I had killed him, but at least he's dead."

That gun's looking more and more appealing to me. I could kill him before they killed me, and that might be okay with me right now. He sees me looking at the gun.

"The gun is for you. It's loaded. If you want to kill me, it's fine. I'm in my last months anyway. My soldiers will kill you though. It would be a fitting end for both of us. Don't you think?"

I'm just staring at him, trying not to tell him too much with my expression.

"I would never kill you. I had my chance when you were a baby. I couldn't do it then, and I can't do it now. I loved your mother more than anyone on earth. I don't care about you. You're obviously one of them now, but I would never do that to Nejra."

He pauses and pulls a picture out of his pocket, and slides it across the table to me. It's a picture of a family—parents and two kids. The kids are around ten years old.

"That's my family. My parents, Nejra and me. We had such happy times before the war."

His voice fades off as he stands up and walks over to a desk. He picks up a framed picture and puts it on the table in front of me.

"This is Nejra about a year before she died, before she met

229

your dad, before she changed our lives forever. She was a silly girl. Never serious about anything. I was like that before our parents died, but she stayed like that. My heart closed the day they died, but her heart seemed to open even more. It was like my parents' spirits shone through her. I might have gotten to that point, too, if she hadn't died. If she hadn't been murdered."

"Do you believe Haroun Hadzic killed her?" My voice makes him jump a little. I don't think he expected me to speak anymore.

"So, you are curious. I was beginning to wonder," he says smiling. "Yes, he killed her. It's amazing the clarity and honesty that you get right before you're going to die. I'm feeling that right now. Are you?"

I'm back to staring at him. Nothing I say is going to matter much now anyway. It's clear to me that I'm going to die in this house.

"Back to being silent. That's fine. I don't have much more to say myself. What's your name now? Millie? I'm not sure what kind of name that is. Nejra named you Yasmine. That was my mother's name. Much prettier than your name, but you don't deserve that name now. You seem to be much more your father's daughter than your mother's. Nejra always told me that she wanted to marry a tender man. I never really knew what that meant. Was your father tender?"

The most tender man ever to walk the earth, but you don't deserve to know that. You don't deserve to even speak about him. As I sit staring at him, I hear what sounds like fire-crackers going off outside. I turn to look out the window. As I'm doing that, the armed men rush in the room.

"Are they here then?" Sayid asks without turning around to look at them.

They respond to him in a language I don't understand, maybe Urdu. Sayid hasn't taken his eyes off me. He responds back to them in whatever language they're speaking. They hesitantly turn around and leave the room, closing the door.

"It looks like our time together has almost come to an end," he says, reaching over and taking the gun off the table. "How did you signal to your friends that we are here? Well, you're a clever girl just like your mother was."

I hear a loud explosion, and now the sound of gunfire is coming from inside the house. It sounds like an entire army is now storming in downstairs. My mind suddenly goes to Mason. I wonder if it's him, if it's his team. I wonder if I'm going to be alive by the time they get here. I don't think I will. I imagine him seeing my dead body as he enters the room, and despite every effort to prevent it, I feel my eyes starting to water. Before I can consider it anymore, I hear voices speaking English in the hallway. It sounds like they're clearing the rooms down the hall, and getting closer to this room.

"He has a gun! Don't come in!" I scream hoping whoever is outside will hear me. "He has a gun!"

Sayid clicks off the safety on the gun just as I hear the door being kicked open behind me. I glance at the door and then back at Sayid, just in time to see him put the gun in his mouth and pull the trigger. A volley of rifle fire riddles his body at the same time. His body slumps on the chair, blood spilling out from everywhere.

"Millie?" I hear behind me. It's not Mason's voice.

I turn around to see an entire team of operators with guns

trained around the room and Chase, in full battle gear, walking up behind them.

"Chase?"

"Yeah, sweetie, it's me. You're okay. We just need to get you out of here. Okay?"

"How did you find me?"

"Culver called me, and told me what you were doing. I've been watching you for a few days now. You almost lost me when you went jogging by yourself. I didn't expect you to do something that stupid," he says, pausing and smiling at me. "But, then you are your dad's daughter. We picked up your cell phone signal after the guards told us you left. Culver had a team standing by."

The tears start coming to my eyes again. I try to stop them, but I can't. Chase pulls me out of the chair and hugs me. "You're going to be fine, Millie. It's over now."

"Ma'am," one of the operators says to me. "Is this Custovic?"

He's pointing at the body. It snaps me out of my fog. I still have a job to do.

"Yes, we need to bring his body back to get a hundred percent ID. Also, Yusef Hadzic's body is downstairs. I'll show you which one he is. A picture ID should do."

I walk through the house with the team, showing them which of the now-dead men seemed to be in Sayid's inner circle including Yusef. They take pictures of all of the dead bodies and collect the computers and files in the house. Chase has not let me move more than a foot from his body since they rescued me. He leads me out to the helicopter, helps me in, and puts his arm around me.

"Your dad would be so proud of you, Millie. He is so proud. I know it," he whispers to me as the helicopter takes off.

Epilogue

MILLIE, SAN DIEGO, CALIFORNIA, 2020

It's been nearly four months since I left Bosnia, and even though I've thought about Mason almost every second of every day, I haven't talked to him once. I know he was on deployment in Afghanistan until about a month ago, but I haven't heard from him since he got back, and I haven't reached out to him.

I haven't really heard anything from anyone in Virginia Beach except for Culver. He called me a few times to make sure I was okay. And Raine has been blowing up my phone for the last two weeks, but I haven't replied. I'm not sure I want to get an update on what's going on over there with the team, with Mason. I'm not ready to talk about everything. At least not yet.

After I got back from Bosnia, I took leave from the agency. They very reluctantly gave me as long as I needed. I guess when you pull in two whales as big as Custovic and Hadzic, you get whatever you want. It hasn't stopped George from calling me every week, trying to convince me to come back to D.C. He said they want me to work in the field now. I haven't answered him.

I moved out of my apartment in D.C., and sold Camille's house and land. I can't believe how much money I got from that sale. I wonder if Camille knew how much it was worth. I decided to finally go ahead with the plan that Dad and I had before he died. I moved to San Diego and bought a house a few blocks off Pacific Beach.

I think about Dad a lot, but like Mason told me it would, it's getting a little easier. I still miss Dad so much, but the memories of him warm me now, more often than they hurt me. Some of his old team buddies, including Chase, live out here. They've taken me into their group and although I was more than a little reluctant to join their family at first, I've come to look forward to the barbecues and birthday parties. Mason was right again. I need a team, and these guys are some great teammates.

I'm trying to decide what to do next, but my mind isn't letting me go there right now. Even after four months, all it wants to let me do is sleep and surf. I'm trying to feel all of the emotions now instead of burying them. Chase told me the grieving process takes whatever time it takes, and that I have to honor it. I know he's talking about Dad, and I am still grieving him, but I'm grieving Mason, too.

"Millie?" I hear coming from my front door. Speaking of Chase. He texted me this morning and said he was coming over to work on something. He's taken on my rundown, little beach bungalow as his latest project.

"Hey, Chase. I'm in the bedroom. Be right out," I shout over Clapton playing loudly from the front room.

"Hey, you going surfing?" He's standing in the kitchen eating the cookies I made last night.

"Yeah. I'm not sure how good the surf is, but I thought I'd go out for a little bit anyway. What are you working on today?"

"I'm installing an automatic lock on your back gate, so it locks when you close it because I know you can't be bothered to do it manually," he says, full of fatherly disdain.

"Chase, it's not needed. Even if someone comes into the backyard, they can't get in the house. I always lock the house."

"Yeah, and when you're using the outdoor shower after you get back from the beach? It gives them plenty of time to attack you."

"You sound just like Dad. No one is going to attack me in Pacific Beach, but if you want to make this place an impenetrable fortress, knock yourself out."

"I will do that," he says. "I start digging the moat next week."

I smile and roll my eyes at him, knowing he's probably only half kidding.

"Will you please eat the rest of the cookies? I've already eaten about ten," I say, giving him a kiss on the cheek as I head out back to grab my surfboard.

"Roger that," I hear him say as I type the security code into the back door. He installed that system last month. Seriously, it's getting harder to get into this place than the White House.

I put my board on the rack on my bike, and pedal the three blocks down to the pier. The ocean's completely flat. Not much chance of catching a wave today, but I decide to paddle out past the pier and chill out a while.

I've probably been out here about thirty minutes when I think I hear my name. I look around to all the surfers about a hundred yards over who are trying to catch a ride on the smallest break. I don't think I know any of them, and none of them seem to be looking at me.

I look over to the pier, and I see a guy standing on the railing, waving his arms wildly. I think he's yelling at me. Maybe he's warning me about a shark. I look around for fins. I don't see any, but I pull my legs up instinctively. I look back at the guy just in time to see him do a swan dive off the end of the pier.

He surfaces and starts swimming over to me quickly. He's swimming like he's in an Olympic race. What the hell? I'm about ready to start paddling for shore, when he stops swimming long enough to look over at me. I almost fall off the board when I see Mason's eyes popping out of the water.

Epilogue

I touched down in San Diego about fifteen minutes ago, and I'm already headed to the address Culver gave me for Millie. He gave it to me reluctantly, but he knew I was going to find her no matter what it took. I pull up in front of her house to find some guy opening her back gate. I'm not sure if he's trying to break in, or worse, if he lives there with her.

He looks at me as suspiciously as I look at him as I walk up to the house. He's in decent shape, but he's way too fucking old for her. I'm hoping he's just a handyman.

"I'm looking for Millie. She live here?"

He pumps out his chest and drops the screwdriver he's holding into the toolbox. "Who the fuck are you?"

"Who the fuck are you?" I snap back. I'm ready to fight him if I need to, and let me tell you, he should have kept that screwdriver in his hand.

He stares at me for a good minute before a slight smile starts forming on his face. That's starting to piss me off until he says, "You're Mason, aren't you? Culver told me you were probably coming out."

"Yeah. I'm Mason. Who are you?"

"Chase. I was her dad's best friend."

"You live here with her now?" I ask accusingly.

"Man, don't be an asshole. She's like a daughter to me. My wife and I moved here after I retired," he says, walking toward me. "I'm here right now installing an automatic lock on her back gate because she's too damn stubborn to lock it when she goes surfing."

I shake my head, smiling. "Well, you definitely know Millie."

"Yeah, she's a piece of work, isn't she? Culver said you helped her out of some tight spots. Thanks for that."

"Yeah, just doing my job, you know?"

"I doubt you'd be here if that's all it was," he says, raising his eyebrows.

"Yeah," I say, looking down. "She surfing now?"

"Yeah. She left about fifteen minutes ago. She's usually off Pacific Beach, south of the pier."

"Thanks, man," I say as I walk back toward my car.

He calls after me. "Mason, I know I speak for Millie's dad when I say if you ever hurt her, in any way, I will kill you. Like honestly, I will go to jail if necessary, but I will kill you."

"If that ever happened, I would want you to kill me."

He nods at me and picks up the screwdriver again.

When I get to Pacific Beach, I grab my binoculars and start scanning the surfers south of the pier to see if I can spot her. I finally see her way beyond the break. She's sitting on her board looking out at the horizon.

I walk out to the end of the pier and start yelling her name and waving my arms to get her attention. She finally looks up at me, but she doesn't wave back or make any move to paddle over to me. All right, if this is what it's going to take, then let's do this. I take off my shirt, get up on the railing of the pier, and dive in. I look up a few times as I'm swimming over to her. Her face finally registers some recognition when I get about twenty feet away.

"What are you doing here?" I can't tell if she's happy to see me or not.

"You mean in the ocean or in San Diego?" I've finally made it over to her. I rest my arms on her board.

"How about both?"

"Well, I'm in the ocean because I was standing on the pier, waving my arms like a crazy person to try to get you to paddle in, but your stubborn ass wouldn't do it. So I decided to just come to you."

"Yeah, I saw your high dive," she says, starting to smile. "I didn't know it was you, but I guess I should have figured it out when you did that."

"And, I'm in San Diego because this is where I live now."

"You live here? Since when?"

"Since about an hour ago when I landed in the airport from Virginia."

"Did you transfer to a team out here?"

"No, I retired from the teams, and took a job teaching new recruits in Coronado. I've got a few years until I have twenty and can retire, and I'm going to spend it here, teaching."

"You retired from the teams? Oh my God, Mason. That's huge. I can't believe you're okay with that."

"You know what? This water is fucking cold. Permission to come aboard, Captain?"

"Can you get on the board without dumping me in the water?" She doesn't look convinced.

"Probably not," I say, grabbing her arm and pulling her off the board.

She surfaces and sees me sitting on her board. "That was not nice," she says, laughing.

"Yeah, I think I'm done being nice." I smile as I grab her under her arms and lift her on the board so she's facing me.

She takes a second to squeeze the dripping water out of her hair. "You really quit the teams? I can't believe it."

"Look, Millie. I loved that job. In my mind, I could do it for a hundred years, but eventually my body's going to give out and make me quit anyway. I did it for fifteen years. It's time to have other priorities in my life."

"What other priorities?" She says it so softly, I can barely hear her. I pick up her legs and pull her toward me until her legs are on top of mine, and our bodies are only inches apart.

"You, Millie. You. You're my priority. That's why I moved here. I want to be with you, and I will make any change in my life to make that happen. You can resist me all you want, but I'm going to keep trying. Because this—you and me—is supposed to happen."

"I haven't told you a lot of stuff about me," she says, looking down.

"I know. Why don't we go back to your house, and you can tell me now?" I say, pulling her chin up so she's looking at me. "There's nothing you can say that will make me change my mind. Absolutely nothing."

She smiles that mischievous smile that makes her eyes sparkle. "You think maybe we can talk about it tomorrow? There's a few other things I'd like to do with you first."

"You're in charge," I say softly as my lips start to explore her face.

"I'm in charge? Really? Are you feeling okay? Do you have a fever?" She wraps her legs around my waist, and her arms around my neck.

"Maybe it's time for you to stop talking now, Millie," I say as my lips find hers.

Read More of the Trilogy

What happens to Millie next? Buy the last two books of The Trident Trilogy, *The Only Reason* and *Wild Card*, on Amazon.

Synopsis - The Only Reason

Reality. Who needs it? Definitely not Millie. She's had enough to last a lifetime. In the past six months, she finally found out who killed her mom and took out a terrorist network in the process.

Phew! Enough reality. It's time for a little fantasy. And she's definitely got the right man for that: Navy SEAL Mason —the alpha male with a tender side—who protected her from danger and healed her broken heart. Then he made a life-changing sacrifice just to be near her. Who could ask for anything more?

But two months into living in this blissful bubble, reality strikes again. Millie's boss tells her a shocking secret. It's news Millie has been wanting to hear for almost nine years.

But is it the truth? Or is her boss only dangling this tantalizing tidbit to get her to take on another dangerous mission?

There's only one way to find out—dive headfirst back into reality. But will this decision risk her relationship with Mason? Will she lose the small amount of peace she's been able to find? Is she putting any chance she has of a happily-ever-after ending on hold to chase a ghost?

Author's Note: The synopsis for *Wild Card* is available on Amazon, but don't read it until after you've read *The Only Reason*. Spoiler Alert!

Be social with me!
    Instagram: @donnaschwartzeauthor
    Facebook: @donnaschwartzeauthor
    Twitter: @donnaschwartze

Visit donnaschwartze.com to sign up for my email list. Subscribers get first access to discounts, prizes, and sneak peeks into future books.

Made in the USA
Middletown, DE
18 June 2021

42677357R00151